The doorknob jiggled and the door swung open.

Miles grimaced, wondering if someone had followed him here to harass him or if someone in town had heard about the murder and had come to do…what? Sympathize with him? Tell him he was no longer wanted in town?

The floor squeaked as a woman walked into the office. Shadows hovered around her, and she was shivering, wide-eyed, so pale her skin looked like buttermilk. Faded dirty jeans and a damp long-sleeved T-shirt hung on her frame, and her long dark hair lay in tangles around her cheeks.

Shock bolted through him as he focused on her face. He had to be seeing things. A ghost, maybe?

She looked exactly like his dead wife.

RITA
HERRON

LOOK-ALIKE

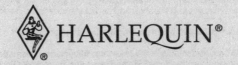

TORONTO • NEW YORK • LONDON
AMSTERDAM • PARIS • SYDNEY • HAMBURG
STOCKHOLM • ATHENS • TOKYO • MILAN • MADRID
PRAGUE • WARSAW • BUDAPEST • AUCKLAND

To my own look-alike—the sweet one, Reba.
May your true love find you and sweep you away!

ISBN-13: 978-0-373-22939-0
ISBN-10:   0-373-22939-9

LOOK-ALIKE

ABOUT THE AUTHOR

Award-winning author Rita Herron wrote her first book when she was twelve, but didn't think real people grew up to be writers. Now she writes so she doesn't have to get a *real* job. A former kindergarten teacher and workshop leader, she traded her storytelling for kids for romance, and writes romantic comedies and romantic suspense. She lives in Georgia with her own romantic hero and three kids. She loves to hear from readers, so please write her at P.O. Box 921225, Norcross, GA 30092-1225, or visit her Web site at www.ritaherron.com.

Books by Rita Herron

CAST OF CHARACTERS

Sheriff Miles Monahue—He's been accused of killing his wife, but when her look-alike surfaces with a bizarre story about being held in a psychiatric ward on Nighthawk Island, will he be able to uncover the truth about which twin is his wife, and find *The Carver?*

Caitlin Collier—She married Miles, then mysteriously disappeared. Did she betray him or was she the victim of something sinister?

Nora Collier—Caitlin's identical twin—is she dead or alive?

The Carver—He believes that marriage means till death do us part, and he has been chosen to dole out the punishment for betraying those vows—with murder. But who is he really?

Federal Agent Reilly Brown—He is determined to get to the bottom of Caitlin Collier's disappearance and find *The Carver*. Will he pin the crime on Miles?

Dr. Hubert Hollinsby—A psychiatrist who specializes in twin identity crisis. Did he conduct experiments on Nora and/or Caitlin? How far will he go to protect his secrets?

Dr. Omar White—He finally convinced CIRP to open another research hospital in Raven's Peak…and he will do anything to keep it open.

Dr. Arthur Mullins—This medical examiner solves crimes through forensic evidence—is he hiding something?

Reverend Perry—His sermons focus on marriage and fidelity—how far will he go to make the people listen?

Buck Bennigan—This cowboy was the last man to see the Collier twin before she died—did he kill her?

Jimmy Joe Johnson—The bartender claims he slept with Caitlin—or was it Nora?

Prologue

"Father, forgive me, for I have sinned."

"And how may I help you, my child?" the priest asked.

"I have taken a woman's life." He stretched his fingers in front of him, the bloodstains still darkening his blunt nails, the scent of the woman's fear still pervading his body.

Behind the curtain, he heard the priest shift uncomfortably, knew he was probably struggling with the need to see his face, with his sacred vows to keep his silence.

But finally, true to his calling, or maybe because his curiosity was spiked, he said, "Go on."

"She is one of many to come," he said, a singsongy note entering his voice. "She was a sinner, a home wrecker. She did not honor her marital vows and she had to pay."

"Only our God can pass judgment on another," the Father said. "We are all sinners. It is not for us to dole out punishments."

Anger, vile and hot, flashed through him. An image of the woman's sultry face followed. Her gaudy makeup. Her whorish laugh. Her wedding ring glittering as she slid into another man's bed. "But there is a secret society of them that has sprung up. They haunt the big cities, the small towns, they are taking over."

"You must turn to God for guidance. Seek help from others who understand your sickness—"

"I am not sick!" He slammed his fist on the wooden surface. "I am a chosen one. I must continue to serve in my own way by ridding the world of evil women."

He stared down at his pinky finger, to her wedding ring. She hadn't deserved to wear it so he had kept it for himself.

And he would have more, so many more, before his work was finished.

Chapter One

"I didn't kill my wife." Sheriff Miles Monahue leaned back in his desk chair in an effort to rein in his volatile emotions. "Like I told the police when I reported Caitlin missing three weeks ago, I have no idea where she is or what happened to her."

FBI agent Reilly Brown's accusing look spoke volumes. "Take off your sunglasses, Sheriff." Brown folded his arms on Monahue's desk and pierced him with a stare as icy as the North Georgia winter wind outside. "I like to look at a man's eyes when I'm talking to him."

Monahue whipped off his Ray-Bans, struggling to bank his temper as he met the agent's gaze head-on. He'd always had dangerous impulses, but lately he'd barely been able to restrain himself from acting on them. He half attributed his springboard reactions to the stress of his wife's disappearance.

But the emptiness had been in his soul a long damn time. And lately, he'd developed severe headaches and a sensitivity to light. The doctor said it was stress, that he needed to lighten up. Release his emotions in a healthy way.

Hell, the man didn't know what he was talking about.

Besides, without the shades, he felt exposed, raw. As if someone might see inside his soul and glimpse the darkness. The bitter boy he'd turned into after he'd witnessed his parents' murder at age ten. The fact that he'd been a suspect in their deaths.

Or the soft spot he'd had for Caitlin. His hand automatically strummed over his pocket where he still carried the charm bracelet he'd bought for her the night he'd proposed—two tiny silver hearts melded together, just as he'd thought theirs had.

What a damn fool he was for believing such nonsense.

"Do you have new evidence? A lead?" Miles asked. God knows he wanted some news. Some closure.

"I'm the interrogator here." Agent Brown's chair squeaked as he shifted his weight. "You're the suspect. You answer the questions."

Miles gritted his teeth. "Dammit, tell me. Have you found her body?"

Brown's eyebrows rose. "Then she is dead?"

"You're twisting my words." Miles bit back a curse. He had no idea if Caitlin were dead or alive. After that last fight, she'd stormed out of their three-week marriage. A few short days after they'd been married, he'd realized his wife wasn't the woman she presented before the I do's. Or the passionate, love-struck woman she'd led him to believe.

She'd been mysterious. Had been hiding something. And when he'd questioned her about her past, her family, she'd clammed up.

For all he knew, she'd faked her death and would let him fry for murder. But where had she gone?

Brown didn't want to hear his suppositions. He'd only think Monahue was making excuses. "You're interrogating me again," he finally replied, "so that makes me wonder if you've found something new."

Brown twisted his mouth into a frown. "Nothing I can reveal."

Miles stood abruptly, his chair hitting the floor. "Then get the hell out. I'm sick of your runaround. If you find her, call me. Or if she contacts me, I'll let you know."

Brown pushed up from the desk, his boots clacking on the wooden surface. He paused in the doorway, pinned him with a warning look. "Don't go anywhere without informing me."

Miles glared at the man's back as he stalked out, then he slammed the desk so hard his stapler flew onto the floor with a clatter. Frustration clawed at him. Even though he and Caitlin had only been married three weeks, their wedding triggered by a drunken night of raw, passionate sex, he'd exhausted every imaginable lead hunting for her.

Of course, the police suspected him. He was the husband. And the last time he'd seen Caitlin, they had fought publicly. She'd shouted that she didn't want to be married to him. That it had been a mistake.

He'd agreed. He knew nothing about love. Family. Commitment. But his pride had smarted and he'd spouted off in anger.

Where was she?

Off in Tahiti with a lover? Sipping margaritas and laughing at the mess she'd left behind? Or had she met with foul play?

Guilt assaulted him as the gruesome possibilities flitted

into his mind. Caitlin, dead at the hands of a madman. Or maybe she'd been kidnapped and was being tortured and was still alive.

If so, every day that passed meant there was less chance of finding her.

He grabbed his keys and headed to his car. He had to get out of the office. Drive someplace and be alone.

Freezing rain and sleet pelted him as he jogged to his Pathfinder, cold air blasting him as he climbed inside and started the engine. He blew on his hands to warm them, hit the gas pedal and soared from the parking lot, gravel churning beneath his tires, sludge and mud spewing. Storm clouds darkened the sky, the sleet creating a steady staccato rhythm as it pinged off the hood and windshield. He flipped on the defroster, grateful for the noise that drowned out his turbulent thoughts as he drove through the small town of Raven's Peak. He tried to focus on the road and his surroundings as he made his nightly rounds, but the nightmares hovered in his mind, tormenting him. After Caitlin had left, the evening blurred. He'd had a headache, then added liquor on top of it. He must have blacked out. Then the nightmares had started. Nightmares that went back to his childhood.

The rugged edges of the mountain peaks and towering hardwoods rose in front of him like ice statues standing guard to the secrets within their massive walls. The canyon below had once been green and lush, sprinkled with wild-flowers and honeysuckle, a haven for the sun as it fought over the jagged gorges. Now, it looked like a brown crater resting at the underbelly of the mountains, like a dark cavern below ground where shadows walked at night, a home for the demons who rested in their evil lairs.

He couldn't shake the interrogation with Brown from

his mind, or the sense that something sinister had happened to his wife. Hell, he did have his dark side, but he hadn't killed Caitlin.

And not a second had gone by that he wasn't plagued with worry about her. The first few days, he'd beaten the streets searching for her, for any clue as to where she might have been, had used all his resources and questioned everyone in Raven's Peak, where he'd first met her at a local honky-tonk, the Steel Toe. But he'd found nothing but questions.

His hands tightened around the steering wheel. The defroster worked overtime to clear the fog from the storm outside, the gears grinding as the tires clutched at black ice. Day by day, he'd assured himself that Caitlin had probably just run off and left him. She was tough. Formidable. She'd obviously decided she'd married him on a whim, that commitment wasn't her style, and ditched him before the ink on their marriage certificate could set permanently.

Still, he'd blamed himself. It was his fault she had left. He hadn't known how to be a husband. She'd needed something he didn't know how to give.

Love.

He'd almost convinced himself he believed that she was coming back, that at least she was alive. Almost…

But the fact that neither he nor the feds had actually turned up any leads on her whereabouts kept his doubts and fears alive.

Streetlights illuminated the town square. Most of the storeowners had long gone for the evening and the citizens were tucked safely in their homes within the city limits, the wooded hills and valleys of the mountains. A safe, small Southern town.

Until he'd brought Caitlin here and she'd disappeared. Now, he wondered if there might be a murderer among them.

Squinting through the sleet, Monahue searched the shadows of the town park for vagrants or unwanteds, then drove past the high school to check for trouble-seeking teenagers, but the street and parking lot were quiet.

The storm grew in intensity as he headed up the mountainside to the house he'd rented, the wind bowing branches on the bare trees that comprised the sloping foothills. Winter had set in to stay, and the holidays were just around the corner, a time for friends and family.

He had neither. In fact, Raven's Peak looked as desolate and empty as Miles felt inside.

He'd find out the truth about everything. If Caitlin had been hurt or killed because of him, he'd get revenge on the person responsible. And if she were alive, well, he'd at least exonerate himself, keep his job and move on with his life.

Either way, he'd never get seriously involved with another woman again.

Nighthawk Island
Savannah, Georgia

SHADOWS FLICKERED around the sterile hospital room, the scent of antiseptic and alcohol nauseating. Rain pounded the roof, the monotonous drone echoing the beat of her heart. Despair threatened to steal her energy, so she forced herself to channel her courage into the will to survive. But she was so confused, she didn't remember her own name. Did she have family somewhere looking for her? A boyfriend, husband?

Caitlin…Nora…

The two names bled together in her mind as if they were one and the same person. Maybe they were. Sometimes the doctor called her Nora. Other times, the nurse had whispered "Good night, Caitlin," to her in the darkness.

"Here you go, sugar, this should help you sleep." Donna, a robust nurse who usually worked nights, handed her a small paper cup holding a pill, then poured her a glass of water from the plastic hospital pitcher.

She cradled the capsule beneath her tongue, took a sip of water and pretended to swallow it. The bitter taste assaulted her senses, her struggle not to let it dissolve warring with the craving for something to sweep her away from the nightmare she'd been living the past few days. Or had it been weeks?

She'd lost all sense of time.

Donna patted her hand in approval, then ambled her bulk to the window and adjusted the shades, drowning out the dwindling light that had tried to cut its way through the fog. "Let me know if you need anything else, dear."

She nodded, a show of obedience earning her another sympathetic smile. Then the nurse bustled by, humming Patsy Cline's "Crazy" beneath her breath as she exited.

She spit the pill into her hand, her socked feet slipping on the cold linoleum as she ran to the potted plant by the window. Hands trembling, she dug a hole in the potting soil and stuffed the capsule below the surface, then packed the dirt tightly over it. The screech of the lock turning on the door, shutting her in, brought a fresh wave of panic.

She didn't belong here.

Not in this mental ward or research hospital, whatever it was. Worse, she couldn't remember how she'd ended up hospitalized. But she'd heard the nurses talking, whispering about the Coastal Island Research Park on Catcall

Island, and the more restricted facility on Nighthawk Island. The place was dark, had secrets. The doctors were conducting strange experiments, ones nobody wanted to talk about.

So why was she locked inside?

She wasn't crazy. She hadn't willingly committed herself for experiments or treatment. She hadn't experienced delusions or heard voices until they'd pumped her full of narcotics. Then the voices had started, the strange terrifying dreams, the cries in the night from down the hall.

Cries from other patients…her own…

She had to escape. Get help.

Caitlin? Nora…

She had a sister somewhere. She felt it, a connection of some kind. But where was she? And why hadn't she come looking for her?

Snack and medicine carts rumbled outside her room, nurses' laughter and voices echoing in the night. Somewhere down the hall a chilling scream pierced the air.

She rushed to the window and inched back the edge of the shade. The murky sky and woods surrounding the hospital cast the island in an ominous gray. Shadows of drooping palm trees flickered through the haze, heavy with rain. How far was she from civilization? If she ran tonight, would she be able to escape the island and find her way to a town somewhere?

Her reflection caught in the window. A ragged, frail woman stared back. Dark purple smudges marred her skin beneath bloodshot eyes. Perspiration beaded her forehead and upper lip. Her stomach cramped into a knot, and she staggered back to bed to rest. Slowly she'd weaned herself from the narcotics, but going cold turkey triggered nasty side effects that had been nearly impossible to battle alone. Sometimes the sweet need for another shot, a pill, anything to alleviate the pain, to help her rest and obliterate reality was so strong she could barely fight it. But if she succumbed to that desperate need, the dreams, the voices, the cries…would start over again. And this time she might not be able to save herself.

Footsteps sounded outside, and she held her breath, grateful when the person bypassed her room and went on to another poor soul. If the nurse discovered Caitlin was dressed, she might guess her plan and warn the doctors and guards.

Then it would be back to solitary confinement, to that room and the chair.

She nestled under the covers, trying to warm herself as she huddled in the darkness. Seconds ticked by, her eyes glued to the wall clock, the only decoration in the near-empty, gray room. Ticktock. Ticktock. A minute passed. Five more. Ten. Thirty.

Finally, the nurses' voices quieted. The halls grew silent. She had to go now while it was dark. Before they returned to make their midnight rounds.

Removing the butter knife she'd stolen from the cafeteria, she slipped from bed and began to undo the screws that bolted the windows into place. One. Two. Slowly she worked, the task painstaking, the rust adding to her problems. Her hands shook and she dropped the utensil, the clatter on the linoleum floor echoing through the stillness of the night.

Her breath caught. She paused, listened. Prayed no one heard. Seconds later, she began her task again. Perspiration trickled down her cheek as she removed the last screw. A sigh escaped her, then she opened the window.

Fresh air.

Inhaling sharply, she hoisted herself onto the window ledge and threw herself through the opening. Her ankle twisted as she hit the hard ground. Ignoring the stabbing pain and the bite of the wind and rain, she ran through the grass and bushes, into the thick, shadowy woods that encased the property like a fortress.

An alarm screeched as she climbed the gate. Guards suddenly burst outside, weapons drawn. Lights flickered on, and shouts rang out. "The gate! There she is!"

Caitlin dropped to the other side, and dashed through the sea oats. The trees were so dense, they shaded any light. She searched the darkness, disoriented. Which way should she run?

"Stop!"

The shouts propelled her forward. Her heart pounding, she dashed through the foliage. Insects buzzed around her face. Her shoes sank into the mushy ground. A hawk swooped up ahead, and the stench of a dead animal and peat added a sickening odor.

She spotted a clearing ahead, and she raced toward it. The sound of water broke through the quiet. The ground suddenly disappeared in front of her. She'd reached a small cliff. She glanced to the left, then the right, but heard voices from both directions. There was no place to run!

Voices echoed behind her again, carrying in the wind, and flashlights scanned the woods. A beam of light caught her in its glare.

"There she is!"

"Stop her!"

She was cornered. The ocean raged below, a good thirty

feet. Her legs threatened to buckle. Someone broke into the clearing. Shouted for her to freeze or he'd shoot.

Terror seized her. She wouldn't go back. She would die inside.

"Please, God, help me." Her heart thundering, she inhaled, then flung herself over the ledge into the roaring waves.

Devil's Ravine
North Georgia

HE SAVORED THE SWEET SMELL of Eve's fear in the shadows that bathed her as she huddled within her tomb. She was a stubborn one, too far gone to save. Too deeply embedded into her harlot ways to admit that the devil had invaded her soul.

God help him, but he wanted her anyway.

Her chin wobbled, and her eyes turned glassy, but she refused to release the tears.

He felt the fine tremors of her body as he trailed his finger over her naked chest, raked the knife blade in the curve of an *A*, the letter he would use to brand her before he took her life.

A smile curved his lips. Yes, she was so alluring, angelic really, exactly like the first Eve who'd tempted Adam. Yet she was worse. She was married. Promised to another.

Only she had forgotten those vows when she'd taken another man to her bed.

"Please don't do this," she whispered.

He cradled her pale hand in his, then slid the simple gold wedding band from her fourth finger. She didn't deserve to wear it.

The marriage decree stated that the union would last forever—*till death do us part.*

Breaking that vow meant she had to be punished.

Miles Monahue would thank him in the end.

Chapter Two

Nighthawk Island

Fear seized Caitlin as she fought the undercurrent, but she forced herself to take a breath and continue swimming. Another stroke. Another. Her clothes felt heavy, weighing her down. How far would it be to the next island? Could she make it?

Then she spotted the small fishing boat. Deserted, tied to the shore by a long rope.

Her pulse raced as she battled the waves and swam toward it. Her arms ached. Her lungs throbbed for air. Her legs felt like numb weights as she kicked and pedaled forward. Finally, she reached the boat and hurled herself inside. She was shivering, but she grabbed the paddle and worked it against the current with all her might.

It seemed like hours as she struggled to reach shore. The night grew darker, colder, her muscles screamed with strain. The strange nighthawk circled above as if hunting for its prey, waiting for her to succumb to exhaustion so he could attack.

Finally, she approached land. Another island. Here,

she'd find help. Get a ride back to civilization and find out why she'd been locked away.

She dragged herself from the boat and slogged through the sand and shells in the darkness. Dizzy with exhaustion, she wove through the long stretches of wooded land until she neared a road. Cold air sliced through her wet clothes, salt water stinging her eyes. A dog howled behind her, and she forced her rubbery legs to take another step. Up ahead, she thought she heard a noise. The whistle of the wind? A rabid dog? Thunder?

Traffic. A car zooming over the slushy pavement.

Panting, she tore through the bramble, jumped over a patch of overgrown weeds and ran onto the highway, waving her arms. She yelled for the driver to stop, but the ancient pickup rattled by, ignoring her, spewing muddy slush. Fighting panic and dizziness, she began to walk along the edge of the road, hopes dwindling as she realized the late hour and weather would prevent travelers from tackling the narrow deserted roads.

Exhaustion intensified her despair, but she reminded herself not to give up hope. Another car would come by. It had to.

One more step. Another.

It seemed as if hours had passed, but finally a noise broke the silence. Tires squealed, brakes churned. An eighteen-wheeler spun around the curve, crossing the center line. She yelled and waved her arms frantically, praying his headlights caught her, that he didn't run her down.

He hit the brakes and gears screeched as he slowed and pulled over to the embankment. The door swung open, and a man's face appeared, shadowed by the smoke-filled cab interior. The strong odor of French fries and sweat wafted from the truck. "Miss, are you all right?"

"Yes, I—" her teeth chattered "—need a ride."

"Your car break down?" He scratched his beard as his eyes scanned the dark deserted stretch of highway.

Had she not been so terrified of getting caught and restrained in that mental ward, she would have been afraid of him. His beefy arms swelled over a thin wife-beater T-shirt, and a plaid flannel shirt hung loose around his beer belly.

Desperate though, she climbed in, grateful for the warmth of the cabin. She only prayed she hadn't escaped one nightmare to be thrust into another.

Raven's Peak
North Georgia

THE PHONE RANG at 5:00 a.m. Before he even answered it, Miles sensed it was bad news.

"Your wife has been saved now, she's repenting for her sins."

His throat closed. "What? Who the hell is this?"

"She was reborn at Devil's Ravine."

A coarse, sinister laugh reverberated over the line, then the phone clicked into silence.

Frantic, Miles hit the call-back feature. Nothing. Dammit. Panic rolled through him in waves as he yanked on his jeans and grabbed a shirt, but his cop instincts kicked in.

He had to go. He headed toward the door. Agent Brown already thought he was guilty of hurting his wife. He'd better cover himself and give him a call.

His fingers shook as he punched in his deputy's num-

ber. He'd let him handle things at his office today while
he dealt with this. Then he phoned the FBI agent.

Seconds later, Agent Brown's voice echoed over the
line. "What is it?"

"I just received an anonymous call," Miles said. "A
man. He said I'd find my wife at Devil's Ravine."

Brown cleared his throat. "Where are you now?"

"At my place. But I'm on my way out the door." He
grabbed his gun and shoved it into his jeans. "It'll take me
about ten minutes to reach the ravine."

"I'll meet you there."

Miles's head spun as he fumbled for his sunglasses
and raced to his car. Images of Caitlin surfaced. Caitlin
with her silky long hair. Caitlin teasing him in bed.

Caitlin lying naked and cold and alone.

Dead.

His pulse pounded as he started his SUV and tore down
the graveled drive. Thankfully the sleet had let up. As
much as he'd told himself he didn't care anymore, that he
never had, emotions clogged his throat. He had loved her.
And maybe she hadn't left him. Maybe someone had kidnapped her and held her all these weeks and she had
prayed he would save her.

But he'd failed.

Guilt suffused him, making his chest tight. The towering pines and hardwoods rushed by in a blur. His tires
squealed, grappling with the slick asphalt as he wound
around the mountain. The steep incline forced him to
downshift and brake, the miles of dense forest and
deserted country roads endless. If a hiker got lost or was
in trouble, they might never be found.

Unless someone alerted the police. Meaning the killer wanted them to find his victim.

Because he felt remorse, or because he liked the game?

A ray of sunshine fought through the gray clouds as he accelerated and maneuvered the narrow dirt road. Bush and trees marred the rest of the way. He'd have to park, and hike to the ravine.

He yanked on his jacket, checked his weapon, climbed from his SUV and scanned the wooded area. Was the caller still around? Was he watching?

Senses on overdrive, he listened for footsteps and began to weave through the dense brush and trees. Barring the wildlife creatures, the squirrels and birds foraging for food, the forest remained asleep. Gravel crunched beneath his boots as he descended the rocky terrain leading into the ravine, rocks skittering down and pinging into the creek below. When he reached the lower bank, he turned in a wide arc and scanned the horizon, the edge of the woods, the cliff above. Vultures soared overhead, a hunter's gunshot reverberating in the distance. Wind blew damp leaves into a cluster.

Where was she?

His gut tight, he forced himself to turn around again, scan the woods, then the water.

Heaven help him. It was her. Caitlin.

She was lying naked in the icy creek, wedged between some rocks, her arms outstretched, her dark hair tangling around her pale face. White lilies floated around her head like a halo. He stepped closer, his gaze drifting over her bruised body.

A stab wound marred her bare chest, the letter *A* carved across her breasts in blood. He choked out a breath. Two murders in Savannah the year before and three in Atlanta had the same MO. The police had dubbed the killer The Carver. Dear God, now he was here in Raven's Peak.

And he had killed Caitlin.

Savannah, Georgia

THE SUN SLITHERED through the dark morning sky as the driver pulled in to a station to get gas. Caitlin saw the sign for Savannah, and vague memories surfaced—she had a sister, she knew she did. They had been close—she felt her presence as if she were here somewhere. Surely her sister had been looking for her. Or did she know Caitlin had been locked in that mental hospital?

The driver climbed from the eighteen-wheeler with a tired grunt and lumbered toward the men's room, and she slid from the seat and ran toward downtown Savannah. Traffic clogged the narrow streets. Signs for River Street goodies, bars and restaurants, and the market floated by while sightseers roamed the squares. A ghost tour through a cemetery caught her eyes, and she glanced at the tombstones, a shiver racing up her spine.

She spotted a local diner and she decided to slip inside and warm up. Maybe get some coffee. Unfortunately, she had no money or ID. Maybe she could offer to wash dishes in exchange. At least she could get a glass of water, sit down and think.

Steam from the griddle sizzled above the den of people as she entered the cafe. She knew she looked ragged so she rushed to the restroom and cleaned up. The scent of coffee, sausages and shrimp grits filled the cramped space. Heat enveloped her as she claimed a corner booth and grabbed a menu.

A waitress wearing a name tag that read *Verna* and a white apron splotched with grease stabbed a pencil behind her ear and glided toward her with coffee, but halted suddenly, her eyes glued to the TV set in the corner. "Oh, my word!" Verna flicked up the volume. "There's been a woman murdered in North Georgia."

Caitlin angled her head to see the set.

"This late-breaking story in now, folks. We're here with Federal Agent Reilly Brown and Sheriff Miles Monahue of Raven's Peak. A young woman's body was discovered this morning in the mountains in an area locals call Devil's Ravine."

He shoved the microphone toward a tall, dark-haired man with black eyes. Behind him several cops combed the woods, others were huddled near the edge of a stream, and a team of paramedics hovered around a gurney. "Sheriff Monahue, did you find the woman's body?"

The man's face looked haunted. "Yes."

"And is it true that the victim is your wife, Caitlin Collier Monahue?"

A shadow fell across the man's face as he bowed his head and nodded. "Yes, we've been searching for her for weeks."

Caitlin gasped. What was he talking about? She was alive. And she didn't know that man at all.

"Was she a victim of The Carver?" the reporter asked.

Sheriff Monahue scrubbed his hand over his beard stubble. "It appears that way, but we'll know more after we investigate."

Caitlin's heart stuttered as the photo of the sheriff's

wife appeared on the screen. No…dear heavens, it couldn't be.

Her palms sweated as more memories churned through her foggy brain. The photo—yes, it *was* her. Caitlin. But *she* wasn't dead.

So who was the woman in the water?

A fleeting image of standing in front of a mirror hit her, and she frowned, then realized that the mirror had not been a mirror at all, but another woman. It had been her sister—her look-alike…they were identical twins.

Dear God, her sister…Caitlin…Nora—Nora was dead….

Nora, the only family she had left. The only person who cared about her.

She doubled over as grief and fear swelled inside her. She was all alone now. And while she'd been locked away, someone had killed her twin.

Raven's Peak, Georgia
Five hours later

THE LAST FEW HOURS had been pure hell.

Miles stood outside his rental house, his stomach knotted, his hands thrust inside his denim jacket to ward off the cold as the crime-scene investigators and Brown searched his house. He'd already succumbed to a DNA swab, had his bootprints taken and turned over the clothes he'd been wearing. Thank God he hadn't given in to the need to touch Caitlin before Brown had arrived, so his hands would be clean.

One of the detectives confiscated his kitchen knives upon arrival and had already bagged them. Miles had noticed the serrated edges on the steak knives and prayed they didn't match the lacerations in her chest. If they did, then someone had been inside his house and had set him up.

But if this were the work of The Carver, it was a ritualistic serial-killer case, not someone with a vendetta against him. The killer probably wouldn't take the time to frame him. He'd want to bask in the glory and attention of his crime.

He slid his Ray-Bans on, then removed a notepad from his pocket and began a list of his possible enemies to question.

Brown cleared his throat as he approached. "We're finished."

Wind whistled through the trees, a gust sending dead leaves raining to the ground. "Will you let me know what the M.E. discovers? I'd like a report."

Brown gave a clipped nod. "Don't leave town. In fact, you should step down as sheriff until this investigation is over."

Miles cut his gaze toward Brown, grateful for the shades protecting his eyes. "I want to find this lunatic as much as you do." He indicated the notepad. "I'm already making a list of all my enemies."

"You think this is about you?"

Miles shrugged. "I don't know, but we can't discount any angle."

"Fax it to me when you complete it. You also know there were other similar cases across the states?"

"Yes, The Carver."

"Then again, you're a cop, you know his MO," Agent Brown snapped. "You could easily have patterned this crime to look like The Carver's work."

Miles cursed. "Or maybe we have a serial killer here in Raven's Peak, and you're wasting everyone's time hassling me."

"Get your deputy to take over your office, Monahue. Do it now."

Brown ran a gloved hand over his tie, then shrugged and walked to his car. His tires chewed gravel as he sped away. Miles strode to his Pathfinder and drove to the sheriff's office to check his computer and talk to his deputy. His deputy agreed to take over, then left to make rounds. Coffee in hand, he logged onto the central database, plugging in the information about the crime scene to cross check across the states for references to the other Carver cases.

While he waited on the computer to process the information, he sipped his coffee, trying to warm his hands, but a deadly cold had seeped all the way to his bones. Seconds later, the data spewed on the screen. So far, the police had no real suspects. They had questioned all the boyfriends, family, husbands of the five victims. The only connection or similarity they'd discovered among the women was that they had all cheated on their husbands. Hmm. The reason The Carver carved the letter *A* on their chests—Adulterer?

In case they did have a copycat here, he entered the names of the men he'd arrested who had possible grievances against him, prioritizing them according to severity of their crimes and sentences. The first two men were lifers, one serving time for murdering his family, the other for brutally raping and killing a teenager. The third one, Armond Rodriguez, who'd been convicted of assault and battery on his wife, had been paroled two days ago. But Caitlin had been missing three weeks. Still, he'd check him out in case he had a friend on the outside who might have helped him. And he didn't yet know if Caitlin had been abducted the day she'd left him or later.

The next prisoner, Ted Ruthers, had been released due to an illness and was supposedly in a hospice program. Hmm. Not him. Unless he'd hired someone to get revenge on Monahue.

The last one, Willie Pinkerton, had escaped jailtime on a technicality, but he was a ruthless bastard who'd been guilty as sin. He'd stabbed an old lady in his apartment complex just because he didn't like old people. The last address he could find on him was in Georgia.

He heard the doorknob jiggle and the door swung open. Miles grimaced, wondering if Brown had followed him here to harass him or if someone in town had heard of the murder and had come to do…what? Sympathize with him? Tell him he was no longer wanted in Raven's Peak?

The floor squeaked as a woman walked into the office. Shadows hovered around her, and she was shivering, wide-eyed, so pale her skin looked like buttermilk. Faded dirty jeans and a damp long sleeved T-shirt hung on her frame, and her long dark hair lay in tangles around her cheeks.

Shock bolted through him as he focused on her face. He had to be seeing things. A ghost, maybe?

She looked exactly like his dead wife.

CAITLIN WAS STILL NUMB with shock and disbelief as she faced the sheriff. The ride she'd hitched to North Georgia had given her plenty of time to think. An overwhelming sense of grief and despair had filled her, along with a hundred questions. She was alone now, and had been in a mental hospital and didn't know why. She'd lost all sense of time, and now her sister was gone, murdered.

She had to find out who had stolen her memories, and who had killed her sister.

Although her brain was still fuzzy about her past, and she couldn't recall the last time she'd seen Nora, she instinctively knew they had been close. And if this sheriff thought Nora was her, maybe he had married Nora instead of her. Maybe Nora had played a twin switch and for some reason used her name. Even more confusing, she had fleeting memories of the doctors calling her Nora, of thinking she *was* Nora…

But she was Caitlin…wasn't she?

The sheriff's rugged face visibly blanched. "What the hell…who are you?"

She gripped her hands beside her as he removed his dark glasses. His black eyes raked over her, assessing, searching. "I'm Caitlin."

He fisted his hands. "That's impossible. I just saw my wife." His harsh voice blazed with accusations. "She was dead."

"I know…I saw the news," Caitlin whispered. "That woman….my look-alike…" Her voice broke with emotions. "That was my sister, Nora."

He shook his head in disbelief. "You're twins?" His nails scraped the wooden desk as he stood, sending a chill down her spine. "If you are Caitlin, where have you been?"

She wet her lips, her legs threatening to buckle. "In the hospital…."

Tension rattled in the air between them. His breath rasped out. Or maybe it was hers. She wasn't sure.

His pained expression mirrored her own anguish, bringing reality crashing back. She was so confused. Why in God's name was this happening?

A dizzy spell swept over her, along with exhaustion and

the remnants of her harrowing escape. The room spun as she fumbled for something to hold on to.

If she were Caitlin and had been married to this man, why didn't she remember him?

REELING WITH SHOCK, Miles captured the woman in his arms to keep her from slithering to the floor. She shivered against him, and he cradled her closer, uncertain whether to kiss her or shake the hell out of her until she admitted the truth about her identity and where she'd been. Was she really Caitlin? And if so, if she had a twin, why hadn't she told him? What hospital had she been in? He'd searched across the Southern states and no one had listed her as a patient.

She whimpered, and he skimmed her face. Whoever she was, something had happened to her. She was suffering from fatigue and malnourishment.

Her hipbones pressed into his thighs as if she'd lost weight, her long dark hair was matted, and her damp clothes clung to her as if she'd been walking through the sleet for days. And those long black lashes that fluttered over her creamy skin glistened with tears.

Although confused as hell, he whispered nonsensical words to comfort her. All lies. He had no idea how things would be okay. A woman he'd thought to be his wife lay dead in the morgue, while he held a carbon copy of her in his arms.

Almost subconsciously, he stroked her back, memorizing her body, searching for some clue that this woman was his wife. That his prayers had been answered and that she'd come back to him alive. That the woman he'd found lying murdered in the creek with lilies floating around her naked body had been someone else. Her look-alike.

Too many unanswered questions clamored in his head, waiting for answers. He'd fallen for Caitlin's act the first go-around. This time, he wouldn't accept anything at face value. Not even her name.

Her slender body convulsed against his. "You're freezing and in shock," he said. "Let me take you to the hospital."

"No!" She jerked away and huddled against the wall. "Please. Don't make me go back there."

He froze, studying her irrational response. Those pale green eyes that had once glowed with passion for him now looked glazed, terrified. "But you need medical care, you—"

"I won't go back." Her teeth chattered and her expression flared into the wild-eyed look of a mad woman. The panic in her tone suggested she would run if he didn't stop her.

Then he'd never get the answers he needed.

She swayed and bumped into the wall, then her head lolled back and her legs buckled. He caught her just before she hit the floor.

His heart pounding, he swung her into his arms, then cradled her to him and hurried to his truck. He cranked up the heat to warm her as he drove up the mountain to his cabin.

Inside, he lay her on his bed and stripped her soggy clothes, the tremors in her body alerting him to the fact that she might be suffering from exposure. On the ride to his cabin, she had stirred, but was disoriented. She'd mumbled something about being locked up, held against her will, drugged out of her mind. But had she taken the drugs first, then slipped into an alternate reality, or were her ramblings evidence of a real-life nightmare?

The sight of her skin so pale, the small bruises on her wrists, ankles and around her waist, shook him to the core. There were needle marks on her arms, too, that resembled track marks.

Caitlin had not been a drug addict. She'd barely even drunk alcohol. At least not until the last week of their short marriage when she'd clung to that bottle of scotch like a lifeline.

What was going on? Had she decided to experiment and wound up in trouble? Had she become addicted and fallen in with some shady characters? Had she been kidnapped and drugged against her will? Was she Caitlin, and the dead woman her sister?

He wrapped a blanket around her, easing it over her arms, and forced her to sip some water. She barely opened her eyes, took a small sip, then collapsed again. His protective instincts kicked in, the guilt he'd harbored the last few weeks returning full force. Had their argument that last night started the wheels in motion that had caused her to end up like this?

He paused, gripping the bed. Did he really believe she was Caitlin? He'd seen the dead woman with his very own eyes. She looked like his wife. But so did this woman.

Whoever she was, she was in trouble. Whether she was his missing wife or his wife's sister or an impostor, he owed it to her to find out what had happened. That trail might lead him to the truth about his wife.

Hating himself for reacting physically to her, he dragged his gaze from her face. But he had been so starved to see her the last few weeks, he pulled a chair close to the bed and studied her, memorizing her features. Her quivering lip needed to be calmed, stroked, kissed. The tremors rippling through her needed soothing. The bruises on her delicate skin needed tending.

Dammit. The lust he'd felt for her still thrived deep

inside him. His sex throbbed for the heaven her body offered, the primal urges that overcame him the first time he'd lain eyes on her, trapping him in its clutches. But other emotions followed—hurt, denial, betrayal.

She had left him high and dry. Had run off without a word, scared him senseless, and left him under suspicion.

He had to have answers.

Jerking himself out of his stupor, he heated more blankets by the fire and wrapped them around her. She moaned and rolled to her side, curling into a fetal position and burying her head beneath the covers. He flexed and unflexed his hands, aching to reach out and hold her again, to confirm that she was alive.

The self-preservation part of him warned him not to. To phone Agent Brown and fill him in on the latest. To call the M.E. and pressure him for an ID. To take this woman's DNA tonight and send it to the lab.

He walked over to the aquarium by the window and stared into the tank, wishing his head was half as clear as that damn water. The tank belonged to Caitlin. He'd never cared for pets, but she had loved the two little tropical fish. Had said they kept her company.

Hell, how had fish been company?

Still, when she'd gone missing he hadn't been able to get rid of them. No, like an idiot, he'd fed them and even found himself talking to them, somehow thinking that if he kept them alive, she'd return to him.

A whimper broke the deafening silence. She rolled to her other side, her face a mask of pain and terror as she stared at him. Tears pooled in those pale green orbs and trickled down her cheeks, dripping onto the covers. She looked small and so damn helpless, it tore at his gut.

He gritted his teeth, stood and faced the fire, reminding himself not to be suckered in by her again. But her anguish was real, and the primal instincts that had drawn him to her in the first place were so strong they overrode the mental warnings screaming in his head. Grimacing, he strode back to her, crawled onto the bed beside her and pulled her in his arms. She tensed, but he whispered for her to rest. Finally she closed her eyes and burrowed against his chest. He rocked her back and forth, savoring the soft weight of her in his embrace and the sultry scent of her femininity as he held her tight.

Tomorrow he'd call the M.E. Tomorrow he'd find the answers. Tonight…tonight he'd hold her and pretend she was his wife.

Devil's Ravine
Midnight

HE COMBED THE DESERTED STREETS of the small town, his heart heavy in his chest. One sinner had met with glory today. But his work wasn't done. There were so many more. Standing on the street corners trussed up in their high heels and short skirts, skin and cleavage flashing boldly for all the world to see. And then there were the others.

Disguised as faithful lovers and wives but cheating like whores.

They filled the bars from Savannah to Atlanta, all the way to the mountains of North Georgia. Even in this small town where Southern hospitality was supposed to breed friendship with your neighbors, sin had taken over. The town had secrets. The friendships had gotten out of control…not friendships at all, but sordid, twisted relationships.

Nausea rifled through him at the realization that he wanted them anyway. But he must fight his own lustful cravings.

He raised the woman's wedding ring and stared at the simple gold band, the circle that represented the unbroken ties that bound woman to man in marriage.

Her marriage had been broken. She had betrayed her vows, flitted from one bed to another.

And she had had to pay.

Just as the others would for their indiscretions.

He entered the church, his head bowed, his face hidden by his hood. He had been raised in the church. He believed in the Bible. Had testified so many times to others and preached sermons on goodness and mercy. On fidelity.

Time to confess his own sins. Receive forgiveness.

Then he'd take another.

Chapter Three

Black Mountain Research Hospital
Near Raven's Peak

"The Collier woman is missing?"

"Yes." Dr. Hubert Hollinsby glared at his coworker, Omar White, as he paced the confines of his office, one hand pressed to his chest where a sharp pain seized him. Their associates had long gone home, but he and White were chained to their lies and had to discuss the matter. *You should have killed her when you had the chance.* "I'd like to know how she escaped."

"It doesn't matter how," Dr. White said in a low, derisive tone. "What matters is the damage she can do to us."

"You mean to *me?*" Hollinsby's chest tightened again as if a vise gripped it from the inside and was twisting the blood vessels into knots. If she figured out the truth about what had happened to her, about his work, and that he'd sent her to Nighthawk Island, it would be the end of his career. Hell, he'd go to jail, and everything he'd struggled to obtain would blow up in smoke. Not to mention the ruin of his personal life…

"My reputation is at stake here, too. The whole damn

hospital's is," White snapped. "I warned you against becoming involved with a patient. You let yourself get personal with a woman and she ruins you."

Hollinsby shot him another murderous look, the visual image of his statement cutting too close. But Nora's lovely face materialized in his mind, and instantaneous lust surged to his groin.

It had been impossible not to get involved with her. She was a sex siren. When she played her sultry song, men traipsed after her as if she'd cast a spell on them just like the children who'd followed the Pied Piper. Good, sane, rational men lost all sense around her. They had to have her—even happily married professionals like himself forgot about their wives. She had even convinced him to join that swingers group, the one that met online.

Hell, maybe he should have conducted a study on Nora's pheromones; maybe there was something in her body chemistry that made a man's sex harden and his brain turn to mush the minute she wiggled that tight little butt of hers.

Sweat trickled down his jaw, his body craving her again. He'd already made several phone calls. "I'll find her and fix everything." He glanced around his cluttered office, to the tops of the stacks of notes, to the computer, to the various research studies and files on his desk. After ten years of study, he'd finally created an amazing, original, unprecedented project that had rocked White's stuffy opinion of him. But now the entire project might be scratched. And all because he'd screwed that damn woman.

White removed his glasses and tucked them into the top of his lab coat. "You'd better fix it fast. If anyone starts nosing around here, you're on your own. This facility is just getting off the ground. In fact, it took me two years to convince the folks at the Coastal Island Research Park to fund a branch here, and I don't intend for it to be shut down because you couldn't keep your pants zipped."

"It was more than that," Hollinsby argued. "And you know it. I had the perfect opportunity to test my theory—"

"Yeah, and you'd better pray your experiment worked. Because if this woman starts remembering things, then you're history around here."

Hollinsby gripped his chest again. If she started remembering things, if she talked, he'd take care of her, then go overseas. Someone there would be interested in his work. And maybe they wouldn't care if he'd ignored ethics in order to achieve the results.

A knock punctuated the tension in the room, and his secretary, Jayne, poked her head inside, a newspaper in her hand. "There's…uh, something you should see, Dr. Hollinsby."

He strode toward her, yanked the paper from her hand and stared at the front page.

"Dead woman found at Devil's Ravine near Raven's Peak. Authorities have identified her as Caitlin Collier…."

The paper fluttered to the floor, the pain splintering his chest like a knife ripping into him. No, it couldn't be….

Caitlin dead?

Or was the woman Nora?

CAITLIN TOSSED AND TURNED in a fitful sleep, trying to escape her nightmares, but she was thrust back into the horror of the past few weeks.

She was running for her life. Someone was following,

chasing her, he was so close.... No, he'd chained her down inside a white room, the walls were closing around her.

Then she was imprisoned on that island again. Gigantic trees blocked her way, the ocean raged below. Then she saw herself lying in that creek. Shadows framed her naked body. Blood dotted her skin and painted the water red. Her eyes were glazed, open in death.

She jerked awake, trembling and disoriented. Where was she? That hospital?

No, the room was dark, the walls made of logs, the embers of a fire glowing from the corner.

Every limb and muscle in her body ached. She hugged the covers tighter, burrowing into the warmth, but fear overwhelmed her as memories of the day before bombarded her.

A low groan rumbled, and she rolled over, her eyes widening, her pulse pounding. A man lay beside her, a scruffy, dark-haired man with beard stubble grazing his cheek, thick brown hair and the blackest eyes she'd ever seen. Eyes that pierced straight through her.

She sank back, then realized in shock that she was naked beneath the quilts. Her hands fisted into the thick covers, a sob welling in her throat.

This man was Sheriff Miles Monahue of Raven's Peak. He had found that other woman's body, had identified it as her. But it was her sister...Nora. Or was she Nora?

A dull pain throbbed inside her chest, then rippled through her. She had walked from one bizarre nightmare into another.

Miles's dark eyebrows lifted, the flare of anger and distrust in his eyes sending a bolt of terror through her.

Could he have had something to do with her confinement in that mental hospital?

Had he taken her there to rot, to be locked up and forgotten? Could he have possibly killed her sister?

EARLY MORNING SHADOWS bathed the cabin as Miles watched the emotions play on the woman's—Caitlin's—face. He had to call her Caitlin just to give her a name, although he realized she might be lying, that she might be the other twin, Nora.

Confusion, fear and wariness riddled her features, triggering his own questions and distrust. One glance downward and she'd realized she was naked. Another second and she knew he had undressed her. And she didn't like it.

"You were going into shock," he said. "I had to warm you up."

"And that's all that happened?"

He grunted. "You think I'd take advantage of a woman who passed out?"

"You…said we were married?"

His gaze met hers, the undeniable flare of uncertainty in her tone hitting him. She didn't believe him.

"I married Caitlin," he said coldly. "Whether you are her or a look-alike, I'm not convinced yet."

His hands balled into fists as he remembered her tone the day she'd walked out on him. He shouldn't want to protect her now, but he did. And that wasn't all he wanted.

"We need to talk." Ignoring her glassy stare and the tension humming between them, he rose and poked at the fire in the adjoining room, well aware her gaze was glued to his back. Sometime during the night, he'd shed his clothes, the heat from the cabin and his own desires making him break into a sweat. He wasn't a man who cared about his body or what anyone thought—except for the fear he put into their eyes when he unleashed his temper.

Willing his morning erection at bay, he dragged on a pair of boxers, strode to the kitchen, made coffee, then carried two mugs back to the bedroom. Caitlin still lay curled on her side, but she'd grabbed his shirt and had shrugged into it. The sight resurrected memories of long sexy nights with her naked beneath him, her long legs wrapped around him. Nights filled with passion...in the beginning.

But their relationship had obviously been built on sex. An illusion of love.

He wouldn't allow his libido to sway him under her spell again. But if their argument had put her in danger, he'd never forgive himself.

He handed her the cup but kept his distance as she propped herself against the pillows. He'd seen the fear on her face when she noticed his naked body in the predawn light. A ripple of alarm had lit her eyes at his jutting sex.

Caitlin had not been daunted by his size.

"Tell me what happened the night we had that argument."

She practically inhaled the coffee, as if she'd been starved for days, and guilt splintered through him. He should feed her first, let her bathe, get dressed, cover that silky skin and naked body from his hungry eyes.

A feeling of self-loathing assaulted him. He was obsessed with wanting her, while she looked as if she'd been through hell and back.

She licked her lips, her voice not quite steady when she spoke. "I don't know what you're talking about."

"Listen, Caitlin—" he hesitated for emphasis "—if you are Caitlin. We were married for three weeks, we had great sex, we had an argument. You walked out. I want to know why."

She tensed at the mention of great sex. At least he had her attention.

But she sipped the coffee again, stalling. He knew it. So did she. Then her gaze landed on the aquarium and her face twisted in thought. "Tigger. Pooh." Her haunted eyes rose to meet his.

"You remember your fish, but not me?" Anger sharpened his words, and she flinched. Great. He was frightening his own wife. And remembering the fish but not him proved just how important he'd been to her.

She stuttered an apology, but she had no explanation. "I'm sorry. I don't understand, either, but I don't remember you or that night," she whispered. "I…just know I woke up a few days…a couple of weeks ago in a psychiatric ward, and I was being drugged." She raked her hair over her shoulder, making his fingers itch to comb through the mass. "I didn't sign myself in to that hellhole, so you must have."

"What?" Her accusation stung. "I told you, *you* walked out on *me*. I've been searching for you for weeks."

She chewed her lower lip, scrutinizing him, yet he didn't think she was lying. Not completely, anyway. Something traumatic had obviously happened to her and he had to get to the bottom of it. "How did you get the track marks?"

She yanked the shirt sleeves over her arms self-consciously. "I…I told you—they drugged me."

"You expect me to believe that?" He scrubbed his hand over the back of his neck. "Listen, Caitlin. This is what I know. You married me, then walked out on me. Two days after you left, I found out you'd hooked up with some guy in a honky-tonk. Maybe he got you strung out, and now you're scared, running back to me for help."

She shook her head, her eyes blurring with tears. "No, that's not true. I wouldn't do drugs, I swear. And I wish I did remember you." Her lips quivered. "Besides, how do I know you're not lying? That you didn't marry Nora and then kill her? That you won't send me back to that awful place?"

He crossed the room to her, studied her with a frown. But the bruises on her skin softened his resolve, and he ended up stroking her palm with his thumb. "I'm not sending you anywhere, not until I learn the truth."

She clutched the edges of his shirt together, looking so vulnerable he wanted to soothe her. "What about my sister? Who killed her?"

His gut clenched as her look-alike's face flashed into his mind. Dammit, he didn't know what to think or do. "The MO looks like the work of a serial killer called The Carver. He's murdered five other women so far, all in the past nine months."

Tension simmered between them. "Will you take me to see her?"

"I'll call the M.E. while you shower." He gestured toward the small bathroom adjacent to the bedroom. "There should be clean towels on the shelf. And you left a few clothes in the closet. Some sweats and jeans and stuff."

She nodded, then slid from the bed and walked toward

the bathroom, hugging his shirt to her. He tracked her movements, searching for a familiar body gesture, something to prove she was his wife.

Seconds later, the shower kicked on and unbidden images of Caitlin naked came to him. He banished them quickly. Needing some distance from her, he sat down at the Formica table in the kitchen and reviewed the files on his missing wife. They'd met two months ago at that honky-tonk in town. It was karaoke night, and she'd danced her way across the stage wearing red sequins, singing "I Will Always Love You" in a sultry, soul-filled voice that had immediately ripped into his gut.

They'd connected instantly. Later that night, he'd seduced her, or had she seduced him? All he remembered was the mind-numbing attraction, the deep hunger that had whispered that he had to have her, the frenzy in the way they'd come together. And for days after, they'd practically stayed in bed. All she had to do was trail her long red fingernails over his abdomen and his sex stirred.

And when she'd talked about opening an arts center for kids, he'd believed she was a family kind of girl. The kind he'd always wanted but never thought he'd deserved.

A few days later, he'd been so drunk on lust and foolish dreams of happily-ever-after that he'd married her at a local Justice of the Peace's office.

Three days later she'd changed. Turned into a different person.

Three weeks after that, she'd disappeared.

What exactly had she wanted from him? Why had she tied the knot?

Hell, why had he?

Too much tequila and a weakness for a sexy woman? Dreams of a family, one to replace the one he'd lost as a kid?

He'd lay off booze and women from now on.

Scraping a hand over his beard stubble, he skimmed the paltry personal information he'd accumulated so far. They hadn't talked about their families, their pasts; they'd been too busy making love. Whispering promises.

When he'd checked her records after she'd disappeared, he'd learned she was an only child. Her parents had died years ago. And when he'd questioned the patrons at the Steel Toe he'd realized that he knew nothing about his wife. That she'd had no intention of settling down with him. She'd been cheating on him from the start, had played him for a fool.

He just didn't know the reason.

Frustrated, he slammed the folder shut. He'd revisit that honky-tonk and question the locals again, especially the bartender. And he'd take Caitlin with him. If she really were suffering from amnesia, the place might trigger her memories.

Knowing he had to call Agent Brown and fill him in, he punched in the man's number. "It's Monahue."

"Yeah?"

"Listen, I want you to come to my place. We have to talk."

"You can't tell me over the phone?"

"No, it's too important." He wanted to see the agent's reaction. See if he could tell the look-alikes apart.

Brown agreed, and they disconnected, then he phoned the M.E.'s office. An image of his wife lying on the cold steel table amidst the medical examiner's tools hit him, churning up more misery. Then he glanced at the imprint of the woman's body in his bed, and his head spun with confusion.

Was the dead woman his wife, or had his wife returned to him, frail and suffering from amnesia?

"LOOK, SHERIFF MONAHUE, I'm backed up, but I'm going to work on her this afternoon." Dr. Arthur Mullins gripped a scalpel in one hand, the phone tucked beneath one ear while he eyed the seventy-five-year-old man who'd lost his life the day before. "I've had bodies stacked up with that pileup on the interstate yesterday. You'll have to be patient."

"You know time is of the essence in a murder case," Miles barked. "Make this one a priority."

"Don't worry, I'll do my job, you do yours."

"Not a problem. But I need extensive DNA testing to verify the woman's identity."

Mullins twisted his mouth in confusion. "I thought you identified her yourself."

"There's been a complication." Miles paused. "I think the woman has a twin. We have to be sure which one of them was murdered, so I'll need dental records checked as well as any medical files we can locate."

Mullins agreed to run every test possible, chewing on the information as he hung up and walked over to the steel slab to study Caitlin Collier. He hadn't been lying about the bodies stacked up; he had his hands full.

The scent of formaldehyde, the drills and saws and instruments he used in his trade, offended some people, even turned their stomachs. But he had always been infatuated with the human body.

Especially the dead ones.

A smile curved his mouth as he lifted the woman's pale, bloodstained, battered hand. He was an expert at his job. He would find out everything he could from this woman's corpse. After all, he worked for the law.

Any evidence he discovered would help them nail her killer.

Chapter Four

As hot water sluiced over Caitlin's skin, she luxuriated in the sensation of being free from the probing eyes of the nurse at the mental institution, who had invaded virtually every aspect of her life, including her personal regimen of bathing. "For all we know, honey, you might try to drown yourself in the shower," the nurse had said.

And she had been tempted to…. Anything to escape the tormenting sessions in that *room.*

Another, deeper kind of agony consumed her. Her hope for finding the truth, and her family, had been the thread that had kept her sane during her ordeal at the hospital.

But now her only surviving family member was dead.

Grief erupted inside her, tearing at her insides. Although she thought she'd cried all her tears the night before, once again sobs wracked her body. She didn't fight the emotions. If Nora was really dead, then a part of her had died as well.

How was it possible that her sister was gone? Fleeting memories of her childhood flashed before her eyes, spotty and confusing, yet she remembered cuddling in bed with her look-alike and whispering in their own secret language, a special way of talking that had allowed them to communicate without their parents, teachers or virtually anyone else understanding their exchanges. A language and closeness she could never share with anyone else.

She struggled for more details of the past, her later years, but she felt as if her memories had been stolen and only tidbits of her life remained, all jumbled together as if they'd been dumped into a big cauldron and stirred, leaving her to piece together the rest. Where had she lived before she'd been admitted into the hospital? How had she wound up restrained in a psych ward? Had Nora even known she'd been missing, or had someone kidnapped her at the same time and kept her hostage?

The fact that Nora had turned up dead the same day she had escaped the mental hospital was bizarre. Did her escape have something to do with her sister's murder? Was it her fault Nora had been killed?

God, no…

She clutched her stomach as guilt assaulted her. She needed Nora, couldn't accept the fact that her actions might have gotten her sister murdered. What if she knew who had killed her sister but she'd blocked out that memory as well?

And how could she survive alone? She and her sister had been so close they were like two halves of the same person.

Bits and pieces of her past sprang back to haunt her, like snippets from someone else's life that she was watching through a camera. The phone calls to Nora that hadn't been returned. The worry that her sister was in trouble.

She soaped her hair, driving her fingers into her scalp, desperately trying to keep the images at bay, but other disturbing ones followed, images of a life that didn't fit with her desire for a family. Images of nights when she'd performed at a smoky bar. Nights she'd drunk too much and partied into the wee hours of the morning. Nights she'd flirted and caroused with men, crawling into a stranger's bed and waking up God knows where.

Men…there had been lots of men.

Was that how she'd met Miles Monahue?

She closed her eyes, willing away the awful feeling that she had done more than that, that she had sold herself for a good time and hurt others in the process. But she'd never hurt Nora…would she?

Panic squeezed the air from her lungs as she struggled to remember more, but a black emptiness swallowed the rest. Her tears finally exhausted, she rinsed her hair, stepped from the shower and wrapped a towel around her, shivering in the chilly air.

She had to understand the reason she'd married Miles Monahue, or if he had married Nora instead. And she'd do whatever necessary to find out what had happened to Nora, and if she were to blame for her sister's death.

THE SHOWER WATER kicked off just as Miles started breakfast. Thank God. It was too damn tempting having Caitlin back in his house, in his bed, in his shower *naked*. He wanted to go to her, throw her on the bed and demand some answers.

Hell, he wanted to strip his clothes, run his hands over her silky skin, taste her spicy wanton lips, sink himself inside her and screw her until she screamed. Then he might just get his fill of her once and for all.

But he couldn't forget the agony she'd put him through the last few weeks, or that her look-alike lay in the morgue with stab wounds through her hands and heart. That Caitlin didn't remember being married to him and had track marks on her arms. That she might not be his wife but a twin, and that his wife might be the one dead.

No, he'd feed her, then pump her for the truth.

A knock jerked him from his task, and he set the eggs and bowl aside. The toaster pinged, but he ignored it and strode to the front door, coffee in hand.

Special Agent Brown stood on the other side, his expression stony and unreadable. "You wanted to talk?"

Miles nodded and gestured for him to follow him to the kitchen nook, well aware Brown anticipated some kind of confession. One he'd never hear from him.

Brown stomped snow from his boots and accepted a cup of coffee with a mumbled thanks.

"I have that list of my enemies." Miles handed him the final version of his research from the day before.

Brown skimmed the paper, then glanced up, eyes narrowed. "Did you make me drive out here for this? You could have faxed it over."

He shrugged, hesitant to tell him about Caitlin. "Have you found out anything more?"

Brown frowned. "As a matter of fact, I did some checking on your wife. Word on the streets is that she had a reputation in the bars in Nashville before she showed up in Raven's Peak."

He sipped his coffee, biting back a reply. He'd stumbled on that info himself after she'd disappeared.

"You don't seem surprised," Brown said.

Miles shifted onto the balls of his feet. If he said he knew, he'd be hammering the nail in his coffin. On the other hand, denial made him look like a fool.

Letting Brown in on Caitlin's arrival could exonerate him, yet he wasn't sure the woman was Caitlin. And her story about being locked in a mental ward would raise more suspicion. But if Brown found out on his own, then it would read as if *he* were hiding information from the feds and only make him look more guilty.

"I've also been studying up on your past," Brown continued. "Witnessing your parents' murder at age ten had to have affected you, especially since you lived with your grandmother after that. She suffered from dementia, right?"

"Yeah, then she died six months later, and I stayed in a group home. So what?"

"So, the perp who killed your parents was your mother's lover."

Miles silently cursed. He knew where Brown was heading with his theory.

"Your father was gunned down in front of you because of your mother's adulterous behavior. Maybe you have some deep-seated hatred of women," Brown continued. "Maybe your wife cheated on you like your mother did your old man, and you decided to make her pay."

"You must be a fan of that new reverend in town." Sarcasm laced Miles's voice. "He's been preaching on marriage and fidelity." The bitterness that had nearly driven him over the edge for years threatened his control.

Brown lifted one eyebrow. "Haven't heard him. But I do know this—your wife's affair gives you motive for murder. So that puts you at the top of my suspect list."

CAITLIN STOOD AT THE EDGE of the door listening to the men's conversation, her nerves strung tight. The sheriff's parents had been murdered when he was ten? This guy Brown was FBI? Did Miles plan to turn her over to them? Were they going to send her back to the mental hospital?

She gripped the door edge, trying to think, but panic zinged through her. Apparently, Miles had been telling the truth about their marriage. But why had she married this man? And how could she have forgotten him?

Even more disturbing, if she had cheated on him, then he had reason to hate her. Reason to have locked her away. Reason to have killed her...or Nora. What if he had drugged her and admitted her to that mental hospital, then Nora had come searching for her, and he'd killed Nora to keep her from exposing what he'd done?

Chill bumps cascaded up her arms. *That puts you at the top of my suspect list,* the FBI agent had said.

If Miles had killed her sister, she needed to get away from him. She could run again. But she had no one else to turn to.

And she couldn't leave without learning what had happened to her twin.

This other man—the FBI agent—might help her. She'd have to take her chances that he wouldn't send her back to that psychiatric ward.

Inhaling a deep breath, she yanked on the sweats she found in the closet, then pushed open the door and inched inside the den.

Both men stared at each other as if they'd engaged in a Mexican standoff, but at the sound of her footsteps, they turned. Miles's gaze skated over her damp hair and body, sending a ripple of sexual awareness down her spine.

A voice whispered in her head, *If he wanted to kill you,*

*why hadn't he done so the night before? Why did he hold
you and comfort you?*

The other man stood close to Miles's height but had
shorter brown hair and a cleft in his chin. He froze, the
shock on his face evident. "Good God, what's going on?"

"She's the reason I called you, Brown."

Agent Brown's head whipped toward Miles, then back
to her. "I don't understand, Monahue."

"She claims she's Caitlin," Miles stated flatly.
"Caitlin, this is Special Agent Reilly Brown. He thinks
I murdered you."

Caitlin gasped at his bold truthfulness, then clasped her
hands together, the intense look Miles shot her a reminder
of the men's discussion—that Caitlin had been cheating
on Miles. Anger, betrayal and hurt simmered in Miles's
deadly calm voice.

Agent Brown cleared his throat. "If she's your wife,
then who's the dead woman in the morgue?"

Miles arched his eyebrows toward her to suggest she
explain. Caitlin shivered, the aching loss still so raw she
had to clear her throat to speak. "My twin sister, Nora."

Brown's questioning look speared Miles. "You didn't
mention that your wife had a twin."

Miles shrugged, his dark eyes still fastened to Caitlin.
"That's because I didn't know anything about her until
she—" he gestured toward her "—walked into my office
last night."

"I saw the story on the television," Caitlin explained in
a broken voice. "I…I came as soon as I did."

"Where have you been the last few weeks?" Brown asked.

"I was hospitalized," Caitlin replied.

"I've already phoned the M.E. to request DNA, medical and dental records to verify her sister's identity," Miles said.

Caitlin flinched. Miles suspected she was lying, that she might not be Caitlin? That she might be Nora, and that Caitlin might be dead…

Or maybe he was angry she'd escaped the mental hospital and returned. Maybe he was worried she'd figure out he had admitted her, and he feared he'd get caught. But if so, why hadn't he killed her last night or driven her back to that mental ward himself? Why had he called the feds?

"Good. We'll need a DNA sample from you, too," Brown said, directing his attention to Caitlin.

She nodded, knowing it was the only way to prove her identity.

"Were you and your twin close?" Brown asked.

Caitlin glanced at Miles and saw him watching her, studying her every move. Again, scattered broken memories bombarded her. The secret language, the sisters huddled together. Then later…bitter fights.

"I asked you if you were close," Agent Brown asked again, more harsh this time.

"Yes…I loved her," Caitlin whispered, knowing that much was true. Although she sensed something had happened between them, something to drive them apart.

"Do you know anyone who would want to hurt your sister?" Agent Brown asked.

Caitlin bit her lip as she struggled to recall conversations between her and Nora. Any mention of a man, a lover, but she drew a blank. In her mind, she saw her and Nora as ten-year-olds. Anything more recent remained a dark empty hole. "No...as far as I know she...she didn't have any enemies."

"She had one—the person who killed her," Brown said. "And I intend to find out who it was."

CAITLIN'S GRIEF and guilt-ridden look tugged at Miles's sympathy. He understood those feelings well. He'd been bombarded by them since the day she'd disappeared. Remembering how weak she'd been the night before, he poured her a cup of coffee, then slipped it into her hands. She sank onto the sofa and gave him a fleeting smile of gratitude. Then she dumped a packet of sweetener into the cup, and swirled it around just as Caitlin used to do.

"When did you last see your sister?" Brown asked.

She cradled the mug in her hands, blowing on the steamy coffee. "I d-don't remember."

Brown propped one foot on the coffee table, leaned over and glared at her. "What do you mean, you don't remember? I thought you said you were close."

Caitlin backed farther into the sofa cushion, her hands trembling.

"She claims she has amnesia," Miles answered for her. "She doesn't remember marrying me, doesn't know what happened to her sister, doesn't know what happened to her the last few weeks."

Brown's eyebrow rose in question. "Amnesia? That's convenient."

Caitlin flinched. "It's the truth. I remember the two of us being together as kids, but nothing later on."

"Did she live here in Raven's Peak?"

Caitlin massaged her temple as if trying to think. "No...I don't think so."

"What about you?" Brown asked. "Where are you from?"

"I...think we grew up in Georgia, near here, in the mountains."

"Her parents are dead," Miles interjected. "After she disappeared, I checked into her past. According to records, the Colliers only had one child."

Brown frowned, and Caitlin gaped at him, her hands knotted. "I don't understand."

"Neither do I," Miles said flatly. "Someone must have tampered with the files."

"If you were so close to your sister, where was she living? And why didn't you report her missing?" Brown asked.

"I told you I don't remember." Frustration laced Caitlin's ragged whisper. "Like I said, I've been in a hospital for the past few weeks."

"When she showed up at my office, she was in shock, dehydrated and disoriented," Miles explained. Hoping to earn her trust, he omitted the part about the track marks.

Brown gave him a skeptical look. "Where were you in the hospital, and why?"

"I...it was in Savannah."

She hesitated, and Miles realized she was holding back, that her story made her sound unstable. He had to wonder if she was. Maybe Caitlin hadn't mentioned her twin because she suffered from mental problems, and she'd been embarrassed.

Brown continued to drill her. "How did you get from Raven's Peak to Savannah?"

She squinted. "I don't know." Frustration filled her voice. "I realize my story sounds crazy," she said in a shaky voice. "But someone locked me in a psychiatric ward. I was on this island, at a research facility. It was off the coast of Savannah."

Brown exhaled. "The Coastal Island Research Park?"

"Yes, on Nighthawk Island."

Brown paced across the room to the window, then turned back to her. "Go on."

"The doctors at the hospital drugged me and kept me locked up. I escaped the night before last and hitched a ride into Savannah." She sipped her coffee, then glanced at Miles with those pale green eyes, imploring him to believe her. "I went in to a diner in Savannah to warm up, and saw the news report about my sister, so I hitched a ride here."

A heartbeat of tension followed, then Brown asked, "What was the name of the doctor who treated you?"

"I…his name is foggy. But a nurse named Donna took care of me most of the time."

"Have you been treated for mental illness before?" Brown asked.

"No." Caitlin stood and squared her shoulders. "I'm not insane. I didn't commit myself to that facility, and I didn't belong there, either."

Miles studied her, wanted to believe her. But her look-alike was dead, and her story sounded far-fetched. Although he had heard about that research park at Nighthawk Island…

Brown shot him a suspicious look. "If you two are lying to cover up something, I'll find out."

"I want the truth as much as you do," Miles said.

Caitlin inhaled sharply. "And so do I. I may not remember the last few months but I loved my sister. She didn't deserve to die like this."

Miles bit back a caustic remark. He had no idea if Caitlin was telling the truth, but she was right. Her sister hadn't deserved to die at the hands of a ruthless serial killer.

Still, the Caitlin he'd married had obviously kept secrets from him.

Secrets that might have led to her hospitalization.

Or to her sister's death.

CAITLIN ALLOWED Special Agent Brown to take a DNA swab from her mouth, but his disbelieving tone had changed her mind about leaving with him.

Then again, what if Miles was dangerous? What if…

No, if Miles had wanted to kill her, he had his chance.

"Both of you stay put," Brown said as he headed to the door. "Ill be in touch. And I will find out the truth."

As Brown left, Miles pivoted away from her, back to the stove, his body rigid. "I'll fix some breakfast."

She started to argue, but his clipped tone warned her not to bother. Her head throbbed as she walked into the den. She studied the fish, remembered watching them, she and Nora making up silly songs about fish when they were little. Then she turned and stared out the window, studied the snowy woods surrounding Miles's cabin, trying to piece together the puzzle of her past.

"It's ready."

Miles's deep voice jerked her from her thoughts, and she joined him in the kitchen. The scene seemed eerily domestic. Had he always cooked, or had she prepared breakfast for him?

He scooped scrambled eggs onto a plate, added toast, jelly and a glass of orange juice. "Sit down at the table, Caitlin, eat something."

Her stomach recoiled. "I'm really not hungry."

"Maybe not," he growled, "but you need to regain your strength. I don't want you passing out again at the medical examiner's office."

Humiliation crawled up her face. She instinctively knew she wasn't a swooner, but last night she'd fallen into this stranger's arms. Then again, withdrawal from the drugs had left her weak.

And he was right. She'd need every ounce of strength she possessed at the morgue.

She sat down across from him, the small space accentuating his big size, his masculine scent. Again, the hominess of the scene struck her. They were eating breakfast together as if they were a normal married couple. But nothing about her life was normal right now.

She forced a bite of the eggs to her mouth, chewing slowly, then washed it down with juice. He wolfed his food in three bites, ate three pieces of toast, then stacked his dishes into the dishwasher and poured himself another mug of coffee. When he returned to the table, he shoved a notepad and pen on the table. "Make a list of all the men you've slept with the last few months."

"What?"

"You say you're Caitlin. After you left me, they told me at the Steel Toe, that you'd been in there with other men. I want names so we can investigate them." His voice hardened. "One of them might have done something to you, something that caused you to have a breakdown and end up in that psych ward."

A flood of emotions consumed her. Horror that he thought she'd brought this trouble on herself. Embarrassment, confusion, self-loathing followed. And doubts niggled at her. She couldn't imagine sleeping around, not with several men....

But more questions nagged at her—again, she wondered if her actions had led to her twin's death.

"I told you and that agent that I don't remember my past. I certainly don't remember..." She let the sentence splinter off as an image of a man in shadows drifted back. The fear she'd felt for the last few months twisted her insides, and she couldn't finish the sentence.

"I don't believe you," Miles said. "And I sure as hell don't trust you."

Her temper sparked. "And I should trust you? I heard Agent Brown say you were a suspect. How do I know that you didn't kill my sister, that you mistook her for me, and you murdered her because you thought I was cheating on you? For all I know, you're keeping me here so you can get rid of me, too."

"Loving women is my style, not killing them." The chair rocked back as Miles stood, the wooden legs banging the floor. He paced across the room like a caged animal, gripping his coffee cup so tightly it suddenly exploded in his hands. Hot coffee sloshed everywhere, spraying on his fingers and jeans, and the jagged glass sliced his palm.

She shrieked and jumped up to grab a cloth. He released a string of expletives, then swung his hand over the sink, turned on the cold water and stuck his hand beneath the spray. Blood oozed from the gashes and mingled with the water, floating down the drain in a pink swirl. She grabbed his hand and wrapped the dishcloth securely around it, adding pressure to stem the blood flow.

His eyes were gritty with anger and some other emotion she couldn't quite read.

"Are you all right?" she whispered.

He simply stared at her, his dark eyes scrutinizing her face. "Who are you?"

She gasped, then wet her lips. "I told you, I'm Caitlin."

His jaw tightened, then he shocked her by reaching behind her head, jerking her to him and lowering his mouth. The minute his lips touched hers, fire sizzled between them. He assaulted her with his kiss, thrusting his tongue around the outer recesses of her mouth until she parted her lips and invited him inside. Then he ravaged her senses, teasing and taunting her with his tongue before savagely deepening the kiss. His hand tangled in the damp strands of her hair as he cupped her head and dragged her closer. His breath burned her cheek, his lips eliciting a storm of need inside her.

Caitlin's body trembled at the hungry possession, flames of desire spreading through her in a wave of erotic torture. She had never felt so desperate to tear off her clothes and be with a man. Had he always stirred her passions like this? Had their relationship been this volatile when they'd first met?

If she had married him, he had touched, loved, caressed and possessed every inch of her in the most intimate way possible. Then why or how had she ever forgotten him? And why in heaven's name would she have deceived him and gone to another man's bed?

Unless she wasn't really Caitlin, unless she was Nora...

Or what if she was Caitlin, and Nora had played a twin switch on him, and Nora had told him she was Caitlin instead of using her own name?

Was it possible that he'd married her twin instead of her? That the woman he'd thought he loved was really Nora? That she didn't remember him because she'd never been in his bed?

Chapter Five

Miles wrenched away from Caitlin, pushed himself backward and stared at her in shock. He'd kissed her to confirm whether or not she was his wife, to convince himself that he no longer had feelings for her.

Instead, heat had erupted between them, a heat so explosive that unwanted emotions pummeled his chest. Torn between disbelief and denial that she really was Caitlin and the realization that he wanted her anyway, he stalked out the door, shoved his sunglasses onto his face, then strode through the woods. A sharp pain pierced his temple, and he cursed, shaking off the snow as his boots pounded brittle grass, weeds and ice. He felt as if he were a bottled keg of ammunition ready to explode.

Was the woman in his house his wife or her look-alike? For a moment, when he'd kissed her, she'd tensed, had been shy, tentative, so like the woman he'd fallen in love with, yet she'd also been frightened at the same time. But seconds later, those timid kisses had turned seductive, and he'd pictured her writhing beneath him in his bed. Naked and sated and whispering his name in the throes of passion, begging for him to make love to her again.

A dark, primitive desire had taken root inside him, and he hadn't been able to let her go. He'd wanted to touch her, to taste her, to punish her for hurting him, for lying to him, for making him believe she'd died, and then for coming back to life.

Hell, who was he kidding? He'd lost control. He'd wanted to drive himself inside her ever since she'd walked in his door the night before.

But she either had a secret agenda or she had been a victim, and he had to figure out which scenario was true.

The roller coaster of emotions he'd been riding since he'd seen that body floating in the water at Devil's Ravine sent his temper surging to the surface. A howl of fury welled inside him, and forest creatures suddenly skittered in fear as if they sensed a dangerous animal in their midst.

A man filled with so much bitterness that he didn't deserve to be loved. One who should have never married. One who was actually the son of the man who'd murdered his parents.

Only the paper hadn't printed that fact because no one knew. Including Agent Brown.

If he did, he'd certainly pin this serial-killer crime on him.

DR. HUBERT HOLLINSBY'S intelligence gave him power over others. He had to wield that power to protect himself.

Thank God he'd had the foresight to keep the twin's identity and her stay at the psychiatric ward under wraps. With only Omar White, his secretary and the special nurse he'd hired aware of her admittance, he should be able to minimize damage control.

He'd already contacted Donna, the nurse he'd hired as Caitlin's private caretaker, and paid her off for her silence. Having a child who needed serious medical attention had been her Achilles' heel, and he had stepped on it with a firm and unbending foot.

Now, for his secretary, Jayne. Her husband had deserted her, leaving her vulnerable and lonely.

A knock punctuated the silence, and he called for her to enter.

"You needed something, Dr. Hollinsby?" Jayne asked.

He blocked his wife's face from his mind, stood and approached Jayne. He'd noticed the passing looks of interest she'd given him. She was newly divorced, attractive in a conservative kind of way. If she'd lose the bun and those high collars, she might be more of a temptress than he'd ever imagined.

Maybe she needed someone to add a little excitement to her life. And he desperately needed her on his side.

"Jayne, you've worked for me for how long now?"

"Three years." A faint blush stained her ivory skin.

Yes, she was pretty enough. And he was a man.

"I appreciate your confidence, your trust, all you do here. You know that, don't you?"

"Yes."

"And you're due a raise?"

Another blush. "Yes."

He inched closer to her, inhaled the sultry scent of her cheap perfume. Maybe he'd add a few gifts to seal the deal. Flowers. Chocolate. Chanel. "I don't think I've ever paid enough attention to you. I tend to get obsessive with my work and forget about the people around me."

"Your work is important," she said. "You're a genius, Dr. Hollinsby. I don't know of any other doctor more dedicated."

His ego swelled along with his sex. Why had he never noticed her admiration? She was obviously infatuated with him. That was the reason she'd relocated to this god-forsaken mountain when he had.

"Thank you, Jayne, but a doctor is only as good as the staff he keeps around him."

He slid a hand to the base of her neck, weaving his fingers into the soft tresses as he massaged her skin. "I don't want to lose you as my coworker, but I can't hide my feelings any longer."

"You don't have to worry about losing me," she whispered.

She tilted her head sideways, the auburn curls falling softly around her face, and he lowered his mouth, first teasing her lips apart with his tongue, then dragging her closer. Seconds later, they tore at each like two wild animals in heat.

He ripped her blouse to her navel, sank his hands over her plump mounds and kneaded them just before he bit the tips. She shimmied from her skirt, and he grinned at the sight of her garter and hose, his hunger growing as he realized her dowdy package had hidden some delicious surprises, such as big breasts and a wet warm body. She thrust her hips forward, unfastened his pants and shoved them to his knees, then stroked him to a stiff peak. His hands skimmed her thighs, opening her to him, and she bucked upward. With a throaty groan, he ripped her panties aside, shoved her back on his desk, then spread her legs and rammed inside her.

Her cry of release splintered the air just as the phone rang.

The shrill noise drowned out her cries, his wife's voice on the machine barely audible as he groaned his own release and pumped himself harder into her, banging her legs against his desk as he mounted her and rode her into oblivion.

CAITLIN WAS STILL TINGLING with sensations evoked by Miles's kiss when he finally returned to the house. He had his Ray-Bans back in place, hiding his eyes, shielding his expression. Heat still flared between them, yet wariness lingered in the air, and he held his powerful body rigid with self-control.

"I'll drive you to town now," he said in a clipped tone. "That is, if you still want to see your sister's body."

Did she? A huge part of her wavered. She didn't want a mental snapshot of Nora's face, pale in death, imprinted in her mind, yet she had to make funeral arrangements and say goodbye. And would she ever truly believe Nora was dead if she didn't identify her herself?

Grief mushroomed inside her again, along with rage, and she nearly doubled over.

"Caitlin?"

Miles reached for her as if he'd read her debilitating reaction, but she stiffened her spine.

How could she accept comfort from a man who obviously detested her? "I...yes, let's go." Summoning courage, she accepted a jacket from him, then followed him to his SUV. The low hum of the heater and defroster cut into the quiet, warming the car, yet the air between them remained chilly with tension as he wound down the mountain toward town.

Snowflakes and ice fluttered to the ground as a breeze whipped through the treetops. The stiff mountain peaks rose in front of her like gigantic steps to the heavens, offering hollows and peaks, jagged ridges and valleys that were both daunting and welcoming, perfect places to hide.

Or to die.

She snuggled deeper into the fur lining of Miles's coat, wondering why she'd made that comparison. Maybe because the stark contrast of the bare limbs and brown tree trunks against the soft white reminded her of death. A faint memory surfaced of her childhood, the haze of her parents' faces floating into the fog. Her mother and father had been killed on a cold, blustery winter day just like today. They'd gotten lost coming home from a weekend skiing trip, then their car had skidded off an icy embankment. They hadn't been found for days. And when they had, their bodies had been frozen.

She had cried for days. But Nora…she didn't remember how she'd reacted….

Cold. Nora had been numb with shock and grief. She hadn't cried once, hadn't talked about them since.

Caitlin had known then that she and her sister had to depend on one another. And they had. Until a few months ago…then something had changed.

The wind whistled through the windows, and she glanced toward Black Mountain. The scenery was just as daunting as the island she'd escaped. She still remembered the fear breathing down her neck the night she'd jumped into the icy water from the island.

The same night her sister had died.

Were the two incidents related?

It seemed too odd of a coincidence if they weren't…. And she wouldn't find out the truth by running from it.

She turned to Miles, hoping he had information to help

her connect the pieces, or at least to trigger her memories. "Where did we get married?"

Miles glanced her way for a brief second, his wary expression cutting her to the bone. "The Justice of the Peace."

"D-did we date very long?"

He made a disgusted sound. "I'm not sure you'd call what we did dating."

She flushed, the sensations stirred from their earlier heated kiss scorching her cheeks. "So, what happened between us? How did we meet?"

His fingers tightened around the steering wheel. "We met in the Steel Toe, a honky-tonk in town. You were singing karaoke one night when I went in."

She struggled to recall the details, but the past few months remained an empty blank. Why could she remember some of the events of her past, of her youth, yet nothing about the past month or the man she'd married?

He cleared his throat. "You walked over to me, singing as if you'd written the lyrics for me, then later…well, we had a fling."

Caitlin twined her fingers together. "How long were we together?"

"A couple of weeks, then we got drunk one night and tied the knot."

Overindulging with alcohol and marrying on a whim… neither seemed like something she would do. "Marriage was my idea or yours?"

He swung his head toward her. "Yours."

Anxiety pinched the muscles in her neck. When they were younger, Nora liked to trick people, switch places. Could he have met Nora in that bar and married her?

But why would Nora marry him? She'd liked to date around, meet different men— The realization came to her suddenly. They had argued about Nora's lifestyle more than once.

So why would she have settled into marriage with Miles? "Did you regret the marriage?"

He grunted. "When you cheated on me, yes."

Caitlin bit her lip, his verbal description painting a picture of her as an appalling, self-centered, deceitful woman. She had obviously hurt him badly. Had he really loved her, or had their marriage simply been the result of a drunken moment?

She stretched her hand out, studied her finger where a wedding band should have been. His simple gold band glittered in the fading sunlight. He still wore it.

"Did I have a ring, Miles?"

His jaw tightened. "Yes." Their gazes locked, the silent implication ringing between them. She wasn't wearing one now—so what had happened to it? Had she removed it or had someone else?

THE REMINDER of Caitlin's missing ring only cemented the realization that she hadn't loved him enough to keep it. Of course, when he'd first found her sister dead, he'd thought the killer had taken it as a trophy. It was another detail of the Carver's MO.

And maybe he had—that is, if the dead woman was his wife.

But her look-alike aroused suspicions—if this woman was Caitlin, his wife, she must have tossed her ring, as she had their short marriage. Unless her story about being forcefully restrained at the psych ward was true, and someone had removed the band.

He had to check out the Nighthawk Island facility.

"I can't help but think my hospital stay and Nora's death have to be related," Caitlin said in a strained voice.

He didn't see the connection, but the timing of the events did seem coincidental.

"Tell me more about our marriage. Something might jog my memories."

"Look," Miles said, steering around a curve. "I don't know what to say. We met in a bar. The woman I married seemed sweet, a little shy. We danced, had a few romantic nights, made love, got hitched, then everything changed."

"Did you love her? I mean…me?"

He sucked in a harsh breath, not wanting to reveal the raw pain her question triggered. Had he loved her? He'd thought he had. He'd wanted her. For the first time in his life, had let himself hope for a real family. That someone might even love him.

"Miles?"

She traced a finger over his hand and he stiffened. "That's not fair," he said in a gruff voice.

"Please, I need to know," she said softly.

He released the breath he'd been holding. "I thought I did," he said. "But…that was before you left."

"What happened? Did I just walk out without an explanation? Did we have an argument?"

"I don't understand what went wrong," he snapped. "You were loving when we married, then three days after the wedding, I went to work, came home and you'd changed. The honeymoon was over. You…told me that you'd made a mistake, that you couldn't settle down with me or any other man. You liked to party, run with men and live your own life." A self-deprecating chuckle followed. "I was a fool not to have seen it sooner."

There, he'd said it. Took the blame because he'd been an idiot. Had let his own desperate need, his craving for her, obliterate common sense.

"I'm sorry for hurting you," she said in such a low voice he almost didn't hear her.

For the second time in one day, he stared at her in confusion. She sounded sincere, but how could he believe her?

The remainder of the ride to the morgue passed in total silence. A sense of trepidation filled him as he parked at the medical examiner's office and escorted Caitlin inside. He felt her tremble as he guided her to the front office, saw her face pale with fear. Identifying a loved one's body was always difficult, but he couldn't imagine facing a reflection of yourself lying in a morgue.

He wasn't looking forward to facing the battered corpse again, either—especially knowing she might be his wife, *still* thought she might be...

Dr. Arthur Mullins, the medical examiner, greeted them in his office. His eyes widened perceptibly at his first sight of Caitlin. "Well, I'll be damned, it is true. You are the spitting image of the woman in my morgue."

She flinched. "I want to see her," Caitlin said in a surprisingly strong voice.

Mullins nodded. "You don't have to view the actual body. We have cameras now, so you can identify her on the television screen."

"No." Caitlin clenched her arms around her waist as if she had to hold herself upright. "I need to see her in person."

A tense second followed. "All right. Then follow me."

Caitlin inhaled, and Miles pressed a hand to the small

of her back. His wife or not, he wouldn't let her face this gruesome task alone.

Mullins led them through a set of double doors into an icy room with whitewashed walls, a sterile, stainless-steel cabinet and table loaded with medical supplies, scalpels, tweezers, petri dishes… Caitlin's—her look-alike's— body lay draped in a sheet on a metal gurney. The smell of death wafted toward him, and Caitlin swayed, obviously feeling the effects.

He gripped her waist and held her tightly, guiding her to the table. Her gaze was glued to the woman's face, her expression strained.

"Nora…" A cry tore from her when she spotted the knife wounds on her sister's hands.

She pressed her hand to her sister's cheek, letting it linger. "God, Nora, who would do this?" Her voice caught. "And what am I going to do without you? How can I go on?"

He pulled her to lean into him, and she gave him a helpless, lost look, tears pooling in her eyes. "We have to find the sick person who killed her, Miles."

Miles's heart wrenched. "I will. I promise."

Her legs buckled, and her body jerked as sobs suddenly wracked her. Miles cradled her closer to him and murmured soothing words as he ushered her out into the front hallway. "Shh, it's okay."

She shook her head against him. "No, it's not. We're twins, Miles. What if someone hurt her because of me?"

He had no answer to that, so he stroked her back, rocking her back and forth.

Finally she pulled away from him and stalked toward the exit, her voice brittle, her eyes wild with emotions. "If she frequented the Steel Toe, maybe this maniac, The

Carver, saw her there. I'll get a job at the bar, use myself as bait."

"Caitlin, no." He jerked her toward him and forced her to face him. "Absolutely not. It's too dangerous."

"I don't care," she snapped, tears streaming down her face. "Don't you understand? I don't care if he kills me now as long as we catch him."

TWILIGHT. The time night fell. The time the depraved slipped into the shadows to steal the light.

He stood beneath the awning of the Raven's Peak Motel and watched the beautiful redhead exit the door nearest the alley. The swirling smoke and booze, the sweat that had oozed off the luncheon crowd in the Steel Toe, had heated his bloodstream with a yearning to drown himself in the erotic textures and scents. The scent of lust, sex, infidelity. Ahh, so toxic. There were sinners in the bar, on the street. Sinners everywhere.

He could not be a part of them.

Yet he was.

The taste of Caitlin's blood still fresh on his fingertips did nothing to alleviate the bitter ache he still possessed for her. He had wanted her even as he'd killed her.

But he had denied himself. He had to prove himself stronger than those who gave in to temptation.

And now this woman was spreading her filth. He recognized her. Her name was Tina. He'd even met her husband.

He'd seen the man's wife in the bar a lot lately. Had found her name among the swingers online.

How many more would he have to sacrifice before this secret swingers group was disbanded?

As many as needed…

He'd tried in Savannah and Atlanta, but those cities were beyond help. He might be able to save this small town, though, might stop the sin from consuming the residents if he took care of it now. He'd moved here to spread the word. To testify against infidelity.

The sound of the redhead's laughter echoed, shrill and evil, mocking his faith.

Even in the fading sunlight and shadows of the awning, her face still glowed from her tryst, her makeup was still smeared from brutal licks and kisses, and her scent would still hold the sticky smell of her lover. She had let the man rut into her and screw her like a common prostitute, and now she dared to carry that scent home to her husband.

She had to be taught a lesson.

Father Flemming would understand. As would the true believers from his church.

She began walking briskly down the street, her bare legs pale and sexy, her heels clicking on the pavement. The first faint touches of moonlight drifted through the shadows, illuminating her silhouette as she wove through the crowd. She lifted her head toward the sky, a seductive catlike smile curving her mouth. Yet fresh snow drifted down in a white fog, dotting her hair and giving her an angelic glow.

But she was no angel. No virgin, either.

He quickened his pace. He'd have to visit Father Flemming again, ask for forgiveness. Lust was a crime. It said so in the Bible, in Job.

He had to share that conviction with the lost.

Tonight, he would start with this one, the beautiful redhead, the adulteress who had strayed. He was her savior.

Chapter Six

Special Agent Brown frowned. What the hell was going on? He'd sent the DNA evidence from the woman at Miles's house to be tested, but the results would take weeks, at least days, even if they did rush it through the labs. But his preliminary investigation into Caitlin Collier Monahue and her sister Nora Collier was most interesting.

"What's wrong, Brown?"

The sound of Special Agent Amelia Adams's voice skated over his nerve endings, arousing those same feelings of lust he battled every time she walked into a room. Bracing himself to look into her soft eyes, he swiveled in his desk chair and glanced toward her, catching the stunning view of her shapely legs. Damn.

"Brown, are you all right?"

He cleared his throat, reminding himself of all the reasons they couldn't get involved. Her marriage. His problems... "What makes you think something's wrong?"

"The expression on your face as you studied that fax."

He dragged his gaze from her leg upward, over the smooth outline of her breasts to her heartshaped face. "You think you figured me out, don't you, Amelia?"

"I'm a behavioral scientist, Brown. It's my job to study body language."

If she could read him that well, she had to know how he felt about her.

"I'm investigating Caitlin Collier and her sister," Brown said, redirecting the conversation. "Caitlin—rather, the woman at Monahue's house who claimed to be Caitlin— said she was held captive at CIRP in a mental ward on Nighthawk Island."

"Nighthawk Island?" Amelia asked. "God, we've been looking into that place for months. Do you think it's possible that she's telling the truth?"

Agent Brown shifted. "I don't know. But I've checked with the mental hospital and they have no records of a Monahue or a Nora Collier ever being admitted. Of course, the research park had been known for its secretive experiments. They could be lying, covering something up."

Agent Adams leaned against his desk, her mouth pursed. "Interesting."

Brown raked his hand through his hair. "Yeah, and it gets better. According to DMV records, the social security office, the hospitals, there's not a single record to substantiate that Caitlin Collier has a sister, much less a twin."

"What are you saying?"

He hissed out a frustrated breath. "That according to my investigation so far, Nora Collier doesn't exist."

FRUSTRATION GNAWED AT Miles as he drove through town for his morning rounds. He wanted to pound the streets of Raven's Peak again, hunt down this killer and take care of him with a vengeance. And Caitlin professed to want to do the same thing.

But if he brought her to the Steel Toe, would he be putting her in more danger?

She might be determined to help now, but she'd also suffered a shocking ordeal the last couple of days and still looked weak and exhausted.

Don't let her get to you, man.

Solve the case so you can return to your position as sheriff. Even though he was temporarily off duty, he still felt a duty to the people he was sworn to protect.

Ironic—did they know *he* was a suspect in the death of his own wife?

No, in the death of his wife's *sister,* a woman he hadn't known existed until a day ago. He had no motive to kill Nora. Unless the woman beside him was Nora....

He rubbed at his temple where a headache pulsed, and noticed that she'd rested against the headrest. Her eyes were closed, and her breathing steady as if she'd fallen asleep. He studied her slender face, the soft curve of her chin, the slight freckle at the corner of her lip. Had it been there before?

He focused on her mouth, willing himself to remember, but looking at her lips only reminded him of the hot kiss they'd shared earlier, derailing him from the job and making it impossible to think about anything but repeating the moment, so he dragged his gaze away. Still, the image of her in his bed jumped to the forefront of his mind, only this time when he removed her clothes and smoothed the blanket over her, she begged him to join her under the covers. And he did.

Lord help him. He had it bad.

She cheated on you, man. She left you high and dry, as a suspect in her disappearance.

But had she left of her own accord? The night they'd argued, had she intended to return? To try and work things out? Had someone kidnapped her and locked her away in that mental institution? Or had they held her, then killed her, and sent her sister back to drive him crazy?

And what about this Nighthawk Island research park? He'd read things about it over the past year. Shady experiments taking place. Murder. Espionage.

His cell phone rang, cutting into his thoughts, and he flipped it open, the gash on his hand from the broken coffee mug stinging. "Sheriff Monahue here."

"Agent Brown."

"Yeah?"

"I checked in to the list of your enemies."

Miles veered onto the square in the center of Raven's Peak, circling the town to make his nightly rounds. "What did you find?"

"The first guy, Armond Rodriguez, has an alibi. His wife."

"The same woman who had him arrested for assault and battery."

"Guess they made up."

"I don't understand women who take back their abusers."

"Me, neither. But it happens all the time."

"What about the other two names on the list?" Miles asked.

"You were right about Ruthers, he's in a hospice program. Barely knows his own name, I think he's too close to death to kill anyone. And his illness came on suddenly. It's not like he had a lot of time to plan anything."

"What about one of his family members? Didn't he have a brother?"

"I'll have someone check that angle." Brown sighed.

"Now, Willie Pinkerton's a different story. That's one bad cuss. He's supposed to be in North Carolina, but none of his family's seen hide nor hair of him since he was paroled. My agents are looking for him now."

"Good." Although the crime in question didn't fit Pinkerton's MO. He wasn't a serial killer.

Brown emitted a long-suffering sigh. "I've also checked your wife's story."

Miles had no patience for games. "And?"

"So far, no one at CIRP or Nighthawk Island claims to know anything about a Caitlin or Nora Collier or Monahue being admitted."

"What?"

"No record on either of them." Brown sighed. "I also haven't been able to find any record that Caitlin Collier had a sister, much less a twin. According to the DMV, social security office and the law enforcement agencies, Nora Collier doesn't exist."

Miles shot a look toward the woman sleeping next to him, and frowned. "What the hell's going on, Brown? I just left the morgue. These two women are definitely related."

"I'm cross-checking to see if one of them might have had an alias, but that doesn't fit with what Caitlin told you. Besides, Miles, we don't even know if the woman with you is Caitlin. Maybe she's some impostor, some woman who had plastic surgery to make herself look like Caitlin. Stranger things have happened at this research park."

Miles chewed over that possibility. "I saw her reaction at the morgue, Brown. I don't think she's faking it. This woman is grief-stricken over her sister's death."

Caitlin moaned and jerked beside him, and he glanced over to see her watching him, the telltale remnants of a nightmare darkening her eyes. She had obviously been traumatized. No one was that good of an actor.

"But she's confused about her identity," Brown said. "Question her, drill her, take her to her old stomping ground and see how she reacts. Hell, take her to bed if you have to, just find out who she is and what kind of game she's playing." He disconnected the call.

Miles ground his jaw, annoyed at Brown's suggestion. He might be an SOB but he hadn't slept with a woman yet for information, and he refused to start now.

But maybe if he pushed her a little, it would jog her brain, at least trigger her memory of their marriage. Then maybe she could explain why she'd left, and who she'd taken to her bed while she'd been his wife.

That person might be their killer.

He spun the SUV around and drove to the Steel Toe, then parked. Caitlin pushed her tousled hair from her eyes, drawing his attention to the bruises on her arms and wrists. The neon sign advertising the bar splashed red and yellow lines across her face.

"What was that phone call about?"

"Brown checking in. No news yet."

She studied him for a long moment, then nodded, and reached for the door handle. He caught her arm, hesitating, wondering if he should take her home. But they had to unearth the truth.

"We are going in, right?"

She looked so tired she could barely walk, but courage made her lift her chin a notch. His stomach knotted. The last time he'd visited this bar he'd learned that his wife had cheated on him. Was he ready to face her lover if the man recognized her and approached her tonight?

Dammit, he had to.

Then he'd find out everything he could about Nighthawk Island and the work they were doing. And he'd uncover the truth about what they'd done to Caitlin and how her confinement was connected to the serial killer who'd stolen her sister's life.

CAITLIN'S INSIDES churned as they entered the Steel Toe. A huge metal boot sat atop the wooden structure, the name of the bar glittering in white lights. Inside, the room boasted plain wooden floors and picnic-style tables with a winding L-shaped bar that filled one corner. Early afternoon patrons sipped beer and tossed peanut shells to the floor. The scent of beer and cigarette smoke wafted around her. Country music blared from the jukebox while a couple of patrons danced the two-step across the planked floor.

She should remember this bar.

"You were singing here the night we met," Miles said.

Her fingers toyed with her purse strap. Had she seduced Miles? Had he watched her from the bar, offered her a drink? Had the two of them immediately been unable to resist one another?

He leaned into her, taunting her. "Do you remember the song you sang?"

She gritted her teeth. "I don't remember this place at all." But now she wished she did. She wanted Miles to look at her that sultry way again, with heat and want in his eyes.

His mouth curved down into a frown, and he shifted to put himself between her and two husky men who were gawking at her. "You look different now," he said, as he gestured toward a bar stool.

She climbed onto the stool, putting her more at eye level with him, at least with his chest. "How so?"

He tilted his head sideways and removed his dark glasses, letting his eyes roam over her intentionally. "Your clothes, hair, makeup. That night you wore a low-cut, slinky black dress with a slit down the side and red stiletto heels. You were a picture of seduction, a bad girl looking for a good time."

She licked her dry lips, knowing he was goading her. Somehow she couldn't imagine herself intentionally dressing to seduce a stranger. "So, that's the kind of woman you like?" she asked in return.

His mouth hardened. "What man could resist temptation in an erotic package?"

She tried to imagine herself in the outfit he described, knew it would paint a sexy picture, then formed a mental picture of herself flirting from the microphone.

Instead she saw her look-alike. Not her.

Nora had been the showgirl, the entertainer. When they were little, she always performed for company, for their parents, for the kids at school.

She liked jeans and sweaters and…and she didn't like to be the center of attention. Another reason she wondered if Nora had pulled a switch on this man, if he'd really fallen in love with her sister instead of her.

In the midst of the smoky fog, an image came unbidden. A meeting…she and Nora…they had been in the bar together.

"Caitlin?"

She glanced up, and the bartender, a good-looking ruffian-type with a goatee, gaped at her while he wiped the counter.

"Holy crap, sugar," he mumbled, "we thought you were dead. I saw the news report—"

"That was my twin sister, Nora." She shifted and reached for the scotch he placed in front of her, then took a sip and frowned. Miles introduced himself, ordered a whiskey, then explained that they were investigating The Carver serial killer.

The bartender threw his hands up as if indicating he didn't want trouble. "I remember you, man. You talked to me after your wife disappeared."

"Right, Jimmy Joe. And now she's back, but she has amnesia." Miles's jaw tightened. "We're trying to piece together her past, what happened to her the night she disappeared. It was about three weeks ago. We think her disappearance may be related to her sister's murder. Maybe Nora was in here at some point, too. Maybe that night." He gave the bartender the date of Caitlin's disappearance.

"That was the last time I saw her…you," he said, gesturing toward Caitlin. "Or your twin maybe. Heck, I'm confused now."

Caitlin's head was swimming, desperate to connect the two events herself. If her sister had been murdered by the serial killer, and he had locked her in that mental ward, why hadn't he killed her, too?

In the background, "Your Cheating Heart" droned over the speakers as if someone had played it as a reminder of how she'd treated Miles.

A memory emerged through the darkness, fleeting and faint. She and Nora had met here. They'd ordered drinks, sat down together…then the image faded. "Actually, Miles, I think I met Nora here the night I disappeared."

Miles jerked his head toward her. "What?"

"I just remembered," Caitlin said, as she tucked an unruly strand of hair behind her ear. "She called me and asked me to join her here. I…remember us sitting down. It was dark, smoky, the place was packed. We ordered a drink…but then the rest is a fog."

Miles turned to Jimmy Joe. "Did you see the twins together?"

He shook his head. "Are you kidding? I didn't even know she had a twin."

"Did you hook up with one of them?" Miles asked.

The man's eyes flickered away. "Yeah, but, man, it was only one night."

"Which twin?" Miles hissed.

Jimmy Joe hesitated, balling the cloth into a knot. "Caitlin. But maybe it was the other twin. Maybe she was pulling a prank. I've heard twins like to do that."

"Sometimes Nora did like to pull twin switches," Caitlin added, although Miles gave them both a cold look as if he suspected they were inventing excuses.

Caitlin opened her mouth to apologize but clamped it shut. If she had married Miles and cheated on him, no wonder she'd forgotten her identity and the last few months. The more she learned about herself, the less she wanted to remember….

MILES STUDIED Caitlin for signs of recognition, attraction, feeling, anything. But a frown marred her face as if she didn't like their portrayal of her.

Well, hell, neither did he. And what was this about Nora pulling twin switches? Was Caitlin trying to convince him that she hadn't cheated on him? That her sister had pretended to be her, and that Nora was the woman in the bar picking up strangers?

Was it possible?

He grabbed the bartender by the shirt. "Did you do something to one of the twins that night? Maybe slip a mickey into her drink?"

"Naw, man. I was working. Like she said, it was busy."

"Did you see either one of them leave?"

He shook his head again. "No, we had trouble with the soundstage. Orb, the soundstage guy, had his hands full fixing it, and I had mine full because we were a waitress short."

Miles chewed the inside of his cheek. "Who did she hook up with that night?"

"She hooked up with a cowboy named Buck."

"You saw Buck with Caitlin the night she disappeared?"

Sweat beaded on Jimmy Joe's forehead. "Yeah, she had a drink with him."

"Where can we find this cowboy?" Miles asked through gritted teeth.

"He's right over there." Jimmy Joe pointed across the crowd of people to a corner table.

Miles spotted the cowboy just as he vaulted out of his chair and bolted for the back door. Miles launched forward, grabbed him by the collar and pushed him up against the wall near the restroom. Caitlin rushed up behind him. Buck's jaw slackened, his reaction a carbon copy of everyone else's who'd seen Caitlin alive. Or was he shocked to see her because he'd killed her sister himself?

A few patrons paused in their beer-drinking to lean forward. Someone reached for their cell phone, obviously an out-of-towner who didn't know Miles was the law, but

Miles flashed his badge, and the crowd quickly turned back to their own conversations.

"Where the hell do you think you're going, Buck?" Miles snarled.

Buck's nostrils flared, his cowboy hat tipping backward as he reached for Miles's hands to keep him from choking him. "Outside for some air. It was getting stuffy in here."

"What's wrong? Are you surprised to see one of your old girlfriends?"

"I thought she was dead." Buck cut his eyes toward Caitlin, his tone uneasy. "Who are you, lady?"

"Caitlin," she answered quietly. "My sister Nora was killed."

"Then you know why we're here," Miles said, tightening his hold. "You bolting like that doesn't look good, buddy."

"Listen," Buck said, holding up his hands in mock surrender, "I didn't have anything to do with your…I mean your sister's death." His tone softened as he glanced at Caitlin. "You know I'd never hurt anyone, baby. Hurting women is not my game."

Miles's hands knotted tighter, and Buck coughed. "Stop it, man, you're choking me."

Caitlin pressed a hand to Miles's arm, and Miles tensed, but released Buck. Buck staggered back against the wall.

Miles motioned to the front door. "Then you won't mind taking a trip down to the police station to give them your story. And a DNA sample."

Buck glared at him, but obviously realized he had no choice. Miles followed him to the SUV, and Caitlin claimed the backseat as they drove to the station. Maybe the DNA would prove that Buck was their serial killer, although Miles's gut instincts told him the man was a jerk, but not a pathological killer. Buck didn't seem smart enough to pull off six murders without getting caught.

Caitlin's breathing rattled in the tense quiet as he parked at the station. Buck muttered a protest as Miles pushed him into the office.

Miles braced himself to see Brown, who would point out the obvious—the fact that this guy had slept with Caitlin, or possibly Nora, gave him motive and opportunity to kill Caitlin…or to lock her away in a psych ward so she couldn't identify that he'd killed Nora.

A dozen questions hammered at his nerves. Caitlin's comment about Nora liking to pull twin switches disturbed him. What if Nora had entered the bar claiming to be Caitlin? What if she had slept with the cowboy, and Caitlin was telling the truth? What if Caitlin had witnessed the kidnapping, and had a breakdown, then been committed to the hospital?

Or what if the killer had meant to kill Caitlin instead of Nora?

Either way, she was still in danger….

Chapter Seven

Late-night shadows claimed every corner, hiding monsters and evil demons who had come to snatch her.

Caitlin had finally escaped.

And she couldn't go back. No, she wouldn't. She'd let them kill her before they dragged her to that room and subjected her to those awful treatments again.

But she was there. They pinned her down, fastened leather straps around her ankles, her wrists, then something clicked around her neck and head. She screamed but no one heard. The cold, metal probes were pressed to her temple. She felt the jab of the needle, heard the man's low monotonous voice murmuring something...what was he saying?

Caitlin...Nora...

A sea of darkness enveloped her. She welcomed it. Didn't want to be awake. To feel. To know what they were going to do to her.

A soft white light filtered through the darkness. She saw herself when she was small. Her sister was there, holding her hand. They skipped around the backyard, laughing and chasing each other. Tall blades of grass brushed her knees. Wildflowers danced in the breeze.

Then other children gathered around. Laughing. Talking. Shrieking as they formed a line to play a silly game.

Red rover, red rover, send Nora right over.

She glanced sideways at her sister. Her own image stared back.

The children wanted Nora. Not Caitlin.

Nora broke loose, leaving her behind. Caitlin called after her. Nora burst into laughter as she broke the human chain of the children's hands. Then she turned to see Caitlin. Tears glittered in her eyes. Her sister liked to play games, pull twin switches. But sometimes Caitlin didn't want to play.

Then the room spun as if she were on a merry-go-round. This time she was Nora. She had been left on the sideline. The other children grabbed Caitlin's hand, and they circled around, laughing and whispering. Caitlin was the sweet one. She hated her....

She tried to lift her fingers to swipe away the tears, but her hand was tied down. Panic tightened her chest, and she struggled against the bondage, but she couldn't move.

Another sound penetrated the haze. A low whine. Angry voices telling her she was a bad girl. But she wasn't, she loved her sister, she really did....

The memory vanished. In its place, she saw blood. Her sister's hands carved with a knife. Her face pale in death.

"No!"

She jerked awake, trembling and shaking, disoriented. She was Caitlin, not Nora. Wasn't she?

"Caitlin." A man's deep voice registered. She screamed again. He was going to take her back to the room, to strap her down.

Then he shook her. "Caitlin, look at me, it's Miles. It's all right, honey, you're safe now."

She stilled, glanced at the strong blunt fingers curled around her arms, realized she was in bed. Not a hospital bed, but a room in a cabin. Firelight flickered off the man's dark hair and eyes. Black beard stubble grazed his wide jaw, and the tense set to his mouth sent a shiver through her.

Miles. Her husband. A man she barely remembered. But she liked his touch. He was powerful, in control, strong. He would protect her.

"Don't let them get me again," she whispered.

He cupped her face in his hands and stroked her cheek. "No, I won't. You were dreaming, having a nightmare."

"I was there again," she said on a pained sigh. "They were strapping me down, they tied me in this chair and gave me shock treatments." Her heart sputtered. "God, why…why did they do that to me? I'm not crazy, Miles, I swear I'm not…."

He cradled her against him and held her tightly. "I don't know yet, but we'll find out," he said in a husky voice.

She closed her eyes and struggled to believe him. But as much as she needed this man, as much as she wanted to cling to him, if what he said were true, she didn't deserve his affection. She had cheated on him. Even as he held her, she felt the tension coiled inside him, the way he held himself back. He hated her for her lies.

And he would never forgive her.

Just as she would never have her sister back.

MILES HUGGED CAITLIN to him, her cries of terror resurrecting every protective instinct he possessed. Was this woman his wife? And if so, who had erased her sister's identity and why?

"Take her to bed if you have to, just find out who she is." Brown's words taunted him as he stroked Caitlin's back. But he couldn't take advantage of her, not now when she was grief-stricken and helpless....

If you slept with her, would you know the truth? Would you be able to tell if she was Caitlin?

That kiss alone had confused the hell out of him. And now with her body pressed up close to him...

No, he couldn't seduce her. He'd have to wait on DNA, dental records, pray they provided the truth.

Exhausted, he closed his eyes, ordering himself to grab some shut-eye. Tomorrow he had to talk to the people at Nighthawk Island. Brown had worked with the Savannah and Atlanta police departments when The Carver had struck their cities, so he'd look at any suspects they might have uncovered in the other murders.

His phone trilled, and he glanced at the caller ID. Another reporter.

He let the message machine pick it up. He'd have to deal with them sometime, but not tonight.

Still, this town was his to protect. He had to keep the people safe, didn't want them panicking over The Carver. Caitlin moaned, and his gut clenched. He had to discover who had hurt his wife.

And which woman he was married to—the one lying in the morgue or the one in his bed beside him now.

"MILES?"

Early-morning sunlight peeked through the sheer curtains, streaking the pine walls with dappled light, but shadows still claimed most of the room. Miles rolled over, his head throbbing from lack of sleep. Caitlin was snuggled up against him, her warm body pressed against his sex. He moved, strained to put some distance between them, but wound up rolling into the soft spot in the bed toward her instead.

Finally he forced himself to look at her. Her lashes fluttered sleepily, her wide green eyes brimmed with questions and a wariness that suggested she understood the tension humming in his body because she felt it, too.

Double damn.

"Miles, I'm sorry about last night."

"Yeah, no problem."

"Thank you for staying with me," Caitlin whispered. She traced a finger over his chest, and he sucked in a harsh breath.

Her soft, sultry voice tore at him. He cut his eyes over her, wishing like hell he didn't still want her, but dammit, he did. He wasn't even sure he cared who she turned out to be. Caitlin or Nora.

So what kind of bastard did that make him?

The kind who deserved to be fooled by a woman with her own agenda.

But the kind who'd die trying to uncover the truth. If she was a victim, he had to know it. And if so, he'd make whoever hurt her pay.

He swung his legs sideways and stood. "I'll make some coffee."

Without waiting for a reply, he strode to the kitchen, prepared the coffee, then hit the remote to catch the news. Seconds later, Caitlin joined him, looking sexy and rumpled in a soft pink nightshirt. She poured herself a cup of coffee, and he dragged his gaze away. Feeling her naked legs against him had been pure torture.

"This late-breaking story in from WSIB News. Mrs.

Tina Hollinsby, the wife of a psychiatrist at the new Black Mountain Hospital and Research facility, has been reported missing. She was last seen at the Steel Toe around 10:00 p.m., night before last. If you have any news on her whereabouts—"

"Oh, my God," Caitlin gasped.

Miles glanced at Caitlin. She crumpled to the sofa, the color draining from her face.

"What's wrong, Caitlin?"

Her hand trembled as she pointed to the screen. "That doctor. Hollinsby—he's the one who treated me at the mental ward on Nighthawk Island. The one who held me there against my will."

THE MINUTE HUBERT HOLLINSBY climbed from his Mercedes at the hospital, reporters accosted him.

A slender Asian woman shoved a microphone in his face. "Dr. Hollinsby, when did you last see your wife?"

"Did you report her missing?" another reporter shouted.

"Do you think she was murdered like that sheriff's wife?" the third one asked.

"No comment." He threw his hands up to ward off the flash of the camera, ducking behind his briefcase and running up the steps. The reporters swarmed after him, but he managed to dash inside the building, then frantically waved at security to stop the entourage from entering. But one had already snuck into the building. A camera flashed.

A man and woman approached him and identified themselves as Detectives Waylar and Rusch from the Black Mountain Police Department. "We'd like to ask you a few questions," one of them said.

Hollinsby gave a clipped nod, sweat beading on his forehead as he angled his face away from the camera. "Follow me, let's do this in private."

A few minutes later, they were seated in his office. Jayne gave him a concerned look and instantly brought coffee.

"What can I do for you?" Hollinsby asked as he closed his office door.

"We're investigating your wife's disappearance," the female detective said. "Is there a reason you didn't report her missing, that her friend Tammy Waters did?"

"Tammy reported her?"

"Yes. Apparently they were supposed to check in with each other, meet for a cocktail late last night. Tammy grew worried when she couldn't reach her."

Hollinsby drummed his hands on his leg. Hell. He knew where they were going with this. Damn Tina. A scandal with her could ruin his career, prompt more questions, lead to the secrets he was trying so hard not to disclose.

"My wife is very impulsive," he explained. "When she didn't come home, I assumed she'd ventured out on one of her wild shopping sprees and stayed in Atlanta overnight. She wasn't very happy about moving up here in the mountains so far away from the malls."

The detectives traded skeptical looks. "So you and your wife were having marital problems?" Detective Rusch asked.

Hollinsby dabbed at his throat where a drop of perspiration trickled down toward his collar. "No, that's not what I meant." He forced himself to interject a calmness to his voice he didn't feel. "But Tina was…how do you say—needy? She didn't grow up with much, so I spoiled her. Lately, I've been working long hours, and she's been agitated, saying I neglected her." He shook his head. "I'm sure this is all a misunderstanding and when she sees the news, she'll call me, or show up with dozens of packages and an overdrawn credit card."

Detective Waylar gave him a withering look that screamed she was a feminist and hadn't appreciated his assessment of his wife. "We'd like to see those cards. We can check for activity. That might indicate her location."

Hollinsby nodded, and pulled up the account information, then printed it out and handed it to the male cop. He was bound to understand a man's point of view.

But Detective Rusch gave it a perfunctory look, and frowned. "Did your wife have family, any other friends she might call or visit?" he asked.

"No family. Tammy was her only real friend."

"I hate to ask this, Dr. Hollinsby, but could your wife have possibly been seeing another man?" Detective Rusch asked.

Hollinsby's anger flared. Had Tina been cheating on him? After all he'd done for her… "I…not that I'm aware of." He hesitated, then mumbled, "But I suppose it's possible."

Detective Waylar stood and adjusted her jacket. "We'll check out the credit cards and let you know what we find."

Detective Rusch tapped his pen on his pad. "Let us know if or when you hear from her."

"Of course." Hollinsby's heart pounded as the officers closed the door behind them. Where in the world was his wife? And why had she stayed out last night and drawn attention to them when he needed to keep a low profile?

His phone trilled, and he grimaced. It was probably White, panicking over the news attention. He gripped the small handset with sweaty fingers. The last thing they needed was the cops snooping into his personal life. Then they might find out about Caitlin and Nora, and his butt would really be fried....

TINA HOLLINSBY willed herself to be strong, to fight for her life, but she had never been so cold and terrified as she was now.

She struggled to open her eyes, but even as she did, despair swallowed her. She was blindfolded. Naked. Bound and gagged, lying in some sort of an empty room that felt like a prison. The damp earth and stone scraped her bare legs and arms as she twisted to free herself. The steady drip of water echoed in the hollow distance. The stench of body fluids, blood and death seeped through the walls, sending chills down her spine.

Panic rushed to her chest, cutting off the air to her lungs as she remembered the night before. She'd had the time of her life. That cowboy had known how to treat a woman. Not like her husband, who was all quicksilver, in and out before she could even work up a good sweat.

Not the cowboy. No, sirree. He paid attention to detail, to all the right places, had teased her and treated her body as if it were a haven, like a temple where he'd come to worship.

And when she'd finally dragged herself away from his sweating, naked body and left his hotel room, she'd headed back home feeling sated and more alive than she had in ages. She'd wanted to rub her husband's face in it, too. She'd wanted him to smell the other man's sex on her and realize she was still desirable.

But now she might die. All for a good time.

Fear choked her. She'd trusted the wrong person. Had

believed the man she'd met on the street after she'd connected with Buck was a man of the cloth. Had thought he was nice.

But he'd assaulted her, knocked her unconscious, brought her here, stripped her and tied her up. He would be back soon. She knew it. Sickos like him enjoyed taunting their captives. She'd heard about them when she lived on the streets, read about that serial killer who'd murdered the sheriff's wife. Some nut they called The Carver.

Terror overwhelmed her as the details of his crimes hit her. He was supposed to be religious. Just like the man who'd trapped her.

Other scenarios assailed her. Women tortured and raped. Dismembered. Left as food for the depraved.

Why hadn't she remembered the dangers of the streets? She'd thought the small town was different. Friendly. Safe. Especially the locals.

A sob lodged in her throat, and she wiggled her hands, trying desperately to loosen the thick ropes around her wrists, but the cord was so tight, it was cutting off her circulation. A low chanting sound filtered through the haze of fear.

He was back.

The hum of his voice grated through the darkness. More Bible verses. "And yay, though I walk in the valley of the shadow of death, surely goodness and mercy shall follow me all the days of my life."

Tears pricked her eyelids. Would he show mercy on her before he killed her?

Chapter Eight

Caitlin shuddered as the news segment ended. Dr. Hollinsby was real. She had seen him on camera. But he had run from it as if he wanted to hide.

Had he done something sinister to his wife, Tina?

Miles stalked from the bed to the bathroom door. "Let's get dressed. Then we're going to see Dr. Hollinsby and make him explain some things."

"You mean you believe me?" Caitlin asked.

He angled his head sideways and studied her. "I believe that something traumatic happened to you. That you were kidnapped. And if that man has something to do with it or your sister's murder, then he's not going to escape by running from me the way he just did that camera."

His steely voice should have unnerved her, but she sensed his anger was directed at the man who'd hurt her, at Nora's killer, not at her, and she relaxed. For the first time since she'd woken up in that hospital, she felt as if she wasn't alone.

"He gave me injections and shock treatments at that hospital on Nighthawk Island," she said. "He stole three weeks of my life from me as well as my memories." Her voice rose with conviction. "I want to know the reason, Miles. And if he had something to do with Nora's death…"

"We'll find out the truth," he said, his voice lower now, almost soothing.

Her gaze met his and heat rippled between them. A fleeting memory of his hand brushing her cheek surfaced, of him holding her and dancing, and she nearly lost her breath. She wanted to remember more, ached to know if what they had shared was real, if she had loved him.

But even if she did, what good would it do? She had hurt him.

For a moment, he looked as if he were going to come toward her, touch her again, maybe kiss her, but then he exhaled sharply, turned and closed the door to the bathroom.

Disappointment filled her, but she tried to compose herself while Miles showered. Still, her mind wandered.

Would she have followed Miles into the bathroom before? Had they soaped and rinsed each other beneath the warm spray of water? Had they made love with the water sluicing over their bodies?

A slow tingle burned through her at the thought. She imagined his powerful body, his muscles slick with moisture, burning with heat, and a throbbing settled in her core.

Unnerved by her body's response and unable to act on her needs only added to her frustrations over her missing memory and her sister's death. Miles hated her for lying to him, for cheating on him…yet, she couldn't imagine herself deceiving him as he'd said.

And that dream…in the dream, she had been Nora.

Her head spinning with confusion, she tossed aside the

covers and padded to the kitchen for coffee. She had to find the missing pieces of her past and put them together.

Bur first she had to bury her sister.

She swallowed, the tension in her shoulders aching as Miles stalked from the bathroom. His hair was damp, he had a towel wrapped around his waist, his hair-dusted chest wet with moisture. His eyes lingered on the swell of her breasts for a fraction of a second before he tightened his mouth.

"Your turn," he muttered. "I have to check in with my deputy, then we'll head over to that Black Mountain Research Hospital. I want to question Hollinsby this morning."

She hesitated, heard the anger hardening his voice, then pictured Hollinsby's face, and fear rifled through her. "How do I know you won't leave me there?"

He moved toward her so quickly she didn't have time to escape. Then he slid his hand behind her neck, tilting her head back. "You're just going to have to trust me, Caitlin. I want the answers to your identity and your sister's murder as much as you do."

A tense heartbeat stretched between them, and questions rallied in her head. He was a cop, a hard-edged man who seemed to need no one, not a settle-down type of guy.

"Why did you marry me?" she asked.

His dark gaze slid over her, the heat rippling between them palpable. "Because I wanted you," he said gruffly. "I thought…hell, I thought we might make it work."

"But things went wrong," she said.

"Yes, you cheated on me." An angry sigh hissed from his drawn mouth. "Wasn't I man enough for you?"

She flinched at his bitter tone, but hurt laced his voice,

too. Or maybe it was simply masculine pride. An honest answer slipped from her mouth before she could stop herself. "You're more man than anyone I've ever met."

He jerked his head up, as if scrutinizing her face for more lies.

It was true though. If she'd slept around, it had been her own shortcomings, not because Miles wasn't virile, sexy and irresistible. Even with deceit and distrust between them, her mouth watered at the sight of his bare chest and those endlessly dark, mysterious eyes. She felt cold, lonely, as if she'd been alone all her life. And she wanted him to hold her.

"Stop looking at me like that."

"Like what?"

"Like you want me to kiss you again," he growled.

She couldn't deny the obvious. "I can't help it, Miles. I do."

Another heartbeat of silence, and the air was fraught with sexual tension. Images of them naked lying in front of the firelight teased her. His lips tasting hers, his hands playing over her in blissful rapture, his mouth everywhere.

With a muttered curse, he yanked her to him, lowered his head and captured her mouth with his. Instant flames of desire erupted inside her. She moaned and parted her lips, desperate for him to erase the pain she'd lived with since she'd awakened in that psychiatric ward. She was hungry for him, wanted him to make her feel alive, needed, wanted. He could do that, stir her passion to a fever pitch and sate her most wicked desires.

But could he erase the bitter guilt eating at her?

Uncaring that she was playing with fire, she wet her lips, silently pleading with him. As if sensing her message, passion ignited in his eyes. He slid his hands over her shoulders, massaging her neck, then trailed them lower and tore open the buttons to her shirt. With a low moan, he found her bare breasts and cupped them in his palms. His kiss was hot, his touch erotic, the thrusting of his tongue eliciting an ache for more. Then he lowered his mouth and spread kisses down her neck, nipping at her tender flesh until he dipped lower and drew her nipple into his mouth. She threw her head back, moaned and clung to his arms to hold her upright. He kneed her legs apart, slid his thigh between hers, so she felt the pressure of his sex as he pulled her into the vee of his thighs. Hard muscles teased her soft folds, an electric charge surging through her. The sound of his suckling echoed in the room, igniting delicious heady sensations that splintered any remnants of self-control. Then he slid the shirt from her arms until she stood, clad only in a pair of white cotton panties. She suddenly wished she'd worn something sexier, red-hot lacy bikinis or brazen black like…like Nora wore.

He hesitated, looked his fill, swallowed and exhaled as his hand slid between her thighs. She melted into him, wanting nothing more than to sink to the floor and let him make love to her until the sun set and then came up again tomorrow.

But suddenly he bolted away from her, turned and threw his hands on top of his head. "What the hell are we doing?"

She was trembling, quivering with need, with unsated desire. "I…I don't know."

He pivoted, the irises of his eyes on fire as he stared at her burning nipples. "I…we can't do this. Not now. Not until I know the truth."

With another muttered curse, he stormed outside, leaving her standing near-naked, wanting him even more. But even as she ran to the shower to wash off his scent, his words seared her. He hated her, would never forgive her. Would never want her back. Even if she came on bended knees and pleaded with him.

The hot water beat at her face and chest, the yearning inside her growing to a fever pitch. A soul-deep ache to finish what they'd started burned through her. She didn't want to be alone anymore. She had always been alone. Nora had had so many men, but she…

She gripped the soap, her head spinning again. What was she thinking? She had loved her sister. She wasn't jealous of her. Was she?

No. She missed her. But even her sister hadn't been able to fill the void in her life. She'd wanted a man to love her, wanted a family.

And no matter what she'd done, she still wanted Miles for herself.

MILES SLID HIS Ray-Bans on, avoiding eye contact with Caitlin, and silently cursed himself as he drove toward Black Mountain. He had almost lost control back at his cabin. He'd been about to relent and make love to Caitlin.

The call from Brown about there being no Nora Collier troubled him even more. Had someone erased her identity, and why? If this woman wasn't Caitlin, if she was lying to him, what kind of game was she playing?

A fool again, that's what he was. Dragged into her web of seduction just as a fly would be trapped by a bowl of honey.

An image of Caitlin wearing nothing but his shirt came

unbidden, the seductive whisper of her sultry promise urging him to forget the questions, to finish what he'd started earlier.

His temper and common sense offered self-loathing for his weakness.

He had to get a grip. A serial killer might be stalking Raven's Peak and the people in the small community depended on him for their safety. Or at least they used to.

Now his own future depended on finding the truth.

Yet how could he protect them when he hadn't been able to keep his own wife safe? When she was either dead at the hands of a madman or had been locked in a mental ward for weeks without his knowledge?

CAITLIN TWISTED her hands together, studying the cliffs and ridges of the North Georgia Mountains as they drove toward Black Mountain Research Hospital. With every passing mile, she became more agitated. The sound of the motor churning and gears grinding on black ice mirrored the grumbling in her stomach. Acid rose in waves to her throat, the image of that dark hospital room at Nighthawk Island, the cloying odors of antiseptics and body fluids rising through the fog of her memory.

Although her confinement within the walls at Nighthawk Island had been riddled with nightmares and drug-induced images of the doctor, one detail stood out. She had had one primary caretaker. A robust woman named Donna. No other nurses, orderlies, attendants…

Just the nurse and Dr. Hollinsby.

Although his face wasn't clear, the shadowy silhouette of a man leaning over her, injecting her with drugs, repeatedly flashed back. His voice had been gruff, almost hoarse, and low, as if muffled.

And then there had been the mind-numbing shock treatments.

And the screams. Sometimes hers. Sometimes others, echoing through the cavernous halls.

A cold sweat seeped through her, and she burrowed deeper inside her coat, wondering if she'd ever be warm again. The windshield wiper batted at the snow and ice falling as he veered onto the drive leading to the hospital.

He parked, then killed the engine and angled himself toward her. "Do you want to wait in the car?"

"No. If this doctor knows something about Nora, I have to confront him. Besides—" she reached for the door "—what he did to me was wrong. I can't let him get away with it."

He gave her a long, intense look, then nodded, his face a mask as they walked up to the entrance.

MILES SQUARED his shoulders as he introduced himself to the receptionist and explained that he needed to speak to Dr. Hollinsby.

"I'm sorry, sir, but he's not in." She sucked air through her teeth, clearly annoyed. "If this is about his missing wife, the police have already questioned him."

"It's urgent," Miles said. "I need to discuss another matter. It concerns one of his patients."

The young woman shrugged and glanced at a rail-thin nurse wheeling a patient through a set of double doors nearby. "Like I told you, he's not here. And I have no idea when he'll return."

"Then let me speak with your director or the chief of staff."

She nodded reluctantly, then several minutes later, a middle-aged woman appeared and introduced herself as the director, Irene Gailstorm. Miles and Caitlin followed her to a corner office.

"I'd like to help you, Sheriff Monahue," Dr. Gailstorm said as she gestured for them to take a seat, "but Dr. Hollinsby left for the day. Apparently, he was upset about the media attention over his wife's disappearance, couldn't work and went home."

"What kind of work does Dr. Hollinsby do here?"

Dr. Gailstorm smiled. "He's a psychotherapist. He works with patients and conducts research in a number of areas regarding mental health."

"And what areas would that be?"

She shrugged. "Neurological disorders of the brain affecting the frontal lobe. He also has been interested in the behavior of the sociopath."

"Is there a specific project that he's currently researching? Something to do with twins, perhaps?" Miles asked.

"You'd really have to talk to him." She planted her hands on the desk, toying with the edge of a file folder. "Why are you so interested in his work?"

Miles gestured toward Caitlin. "Miss Collier was one of his patients."

She turned her attention to Caitlin. "I see. And you need an appointment?"

"We need to talk to him about her treatment," Miles replied.

"I can have our secretary set you up with an appointment, but in light of his wife's disappearance, I don't expect he'll be seeing patients for a while." Dr. Gailstorm consulted a list on her desk. "Would you like a referral to another doctor?"

Caitlin cleared her throat. "No. I'd like to know why he hospitalized me and drugged me against my will."

Dr. Gailstorm's mouth went slack with shock. "That's absurd, Miss Collier. Dr. Hollinsby is a renowned psychiatrist, a leader in his field. He's one of the most ethical doctors on staff."

"Dr. Hollinsby injected me with drugs, gave me shock treatments and held me in a mental ward on Nighthawk Island in Savannah. He refused to let me contact anyone, not even family."

She offered Caitlin a sympathetic smile, then turned to Miles. "Sheriff, sometimes patients fabricate stories about being restrained, detained against their will, but delusions are usually part of their psychosis. Please let me refer her to another doctor on staff."

"Get Hollinsby on the phone," Miles ordered.

The director frowned, obviously agitated, but punched in a number. Seconds later, she covered the phone with one hand, and said, "He's not answering." She left a brief message, then disconnected. "I'll try his mobile." Lines etched her forehead as she punched in that number, then waited, but apparently the voice mail picked up. "Dr. Hollinsby, this is Dr. Gailstorm. Please call my office as soon as possible. We have a...problem we need to discuss."

Frustration tightened Miles's shoulders. "We'd like to drop by his house. Can you give me his address?"

Another long-winded sigh. "I'm sorry, but I can't divulge that information, Sheriff—"

Miles hit the desk with his fist. "Dammit, lady, this is a police matter. Tell me where the man lives or I'll find out on my own."

Her eyes widened, but she finally accessed her files, then scribbled the address on a notepad.

Miles thanked her, then ushered Caitlin out the door. Inside the car, he punched in Agent Brown's number and explained that Caitlin recognized Hollinsby from the news. "What if he killed his wife?" Miles suggested. "I'm on my way to his house. He might be fleeing the country as we speak."

"No need to go to his house. I'm there now, and he's not home. My agents are checking into flights, the train and bus stations as well. If he's skipping town, we'll catch him." Agent Brown paused. "I'm on my way to interview Mrs. Hollinsby's friend, Tammy Waters."

"We'll meet you there," Miles said. He recited the address, cranked the engine and headed toward the outskirts of Black Mountain.

Dr. Gailstorm's assessment bothered him. Was it possible that Caitlin was lying? That she'd never been in that psych ward, that she'd fabricated this story to gain his attention or sidetrack the investigation? Was he allowing his lust for her, his guilt over her sister's death, to affect his judgment? But if she had been ill and undergoing treatment, why didn't they have records of her at Nighthawk Island?

Then again, if she had mental problems, it might explain her odd behavior, and the lies she'd told before she'd disappeared.

"A FRIEND OF TINA HOLLINSBY'S filed the missing person's report on her," Miles said as they parked in front of a midsized brick apartment complex. The neighborhood looked as if it might have been nice once, but the buildings had aged, the shrubs were overgrown, the white trim paint faded to a muddy brown. "She's a local."

Caitlin nodded and followed him up the sidewalk. A second later, he punched the doorbell, and a young brunette wearing a white T-shirt and jeans answered, her straight hair secured in a ponytail. She looked about twenty-five, although on closer inspection, the wrinkles around her eyes and weariness in them made Caitlin put her closer to thirty.

When she spotted Caitlin, she paled visibly. "You… you're the dead woman in the paper."

Caitlin flinched, wondering if she'd ever recover from losing Nora. "That was my sister."

Tammy offered her a sympathetic look, invited them in, then led them to a small den overflowing with a hodge-podge of furniture. Agent Brown leaned against a bookshelf overflowing with fantasy novels and travel magazines.

"I don't understand what you're doing here," Tammy said. "I've already told the local police everything I know. Have you found Tina?"

"I'm afraid not," Miles said.

"According to the police who spoke with Dr. Hollinsby this morning, he doesn't think his wife is missing," Brown added. "Why don't you tell us exactly what happened yesterday?"

Caitlin and Miles claimed the sofa across from her, while she perched on the edge of the love seat, rocking herself back and forth as if she had an abundance of pent-up energy. Either nerves, or she was high.

"Tina and I met for dinner at the Steel Toe night before last," Tammy said, jiggling her leg up and down. "We usually go there once or twice a week."

"Always on the same day?" Brown asked.

She frowned. "Uh, yes. Usually Tuesday and Friday. Why?"

"We're looking for a pattern. If someone had been watching her, they might have known her routine."

"Oh, good gravy." She rubbed a hand along her neck, jiggling her leg faster. "We were stupid, weren't we? I mean I've heard on the news that women should vary their routines, but we didn't think anything about it."

"No one's passing judgment, Miss Waters," Miles interjected. "We're simply trying to piece together the sequence of the day's events so we can determine what happened to your friend."

"All right, yes, that's what I want." She pressed a hand to her thigh as if she recognized her own nervous habit. "Well, when we were seated, Tina phoned her husband, but he didn't answer. As usual. He's always working and neglecting her, and she was…well, frankly she was pissed."

"That he was working?"

Tammy glanced away as if contemplating her answer. Or a lie.

"Were they having marital problems?" Miles pressed.

She pushed at a strand of hair that had fallen from her ponytail. "She suspected he was cheating on her. She found signs that he had joined this swingers Web site."

"Who was he having an affair with?" Miles asked.

"I don't know. Tina thought he might be involved with one of his patients."

Miles and Agent Brown both glanced at Caitlin. She knotted her fingers together, knowing instinctively that she hadn't slept with Dr. Hollinsby. But would Miles believe her?

"So she decided it was time for payback?" Miles asked.

Tammy bit down on her lip, her nod of affirmation coinciding with another leg jiggle. "I guess so," she said in a defensive tone.

"Who did she hook up with?" Agent Brown asked.

She fiddled with her hair again. "She flirted with this cowboy at the bar. His name was Buck. About a half hour later, she left with him."

"She didn't tell you where they were going?" Brown asked.

"No."

"You assumed they went to a hotel?" Miles asked.

She nodded miserably. "I should have tried to stop her, I guess, but she was having so much fun…" Her voice broke with tears, and she swiped at them, her lower lip quivering.

Agent Brown glanced at Miles. "I'll have someone check the nearby hotels."

Tammy nodded, and Miles, Brown and Caitlin walked to the door.

"Buck is a real ladies' man, frequents the bar," Miles said. "I've already questioned him. His fingerprints are on record. I also ran a background check. He doesn't seem smart enough to be The Carver, but maybe he saw someone with Mrs. Hollinsby." Miles's cell phone trilled, and he accepted the call. "Dr. Mullins? Yeah, we'll be right there."

Caitlin tensed as Miles disconnected the call.

"What's up?" Agent Brown asked.

"He has an ID on the body."

Miles shot her a suspicious look, and uncertainty seeped through Caitlin. She had experienced confusing memories of being Caitlin and of being Nora. And she definitely remembered meeting her sister the night she'd died. What if she'd witnessed her sister's kidnapping, then had a breakdown because of it? Maybe she had sought a therapist for help and Dr. Hollinsby had treated her.

Either way, if the medical examiner had identified her sister, then he knew her true identity as well.

She clenched her hands together as she climbed into Miles's car. Was she Caitlin or Nora?

HER FREEWILL MEANT NOTHING to him. Will had been handed down by the Father. Just as it had been God's will that he serve him by saving the sinners. That he live with death on his hands and hear the whisper of taunting voices as he fell asleep each night. Voices ordering him to rid the world of the wanton women in the town.

He had listened in the confessional today. Had heard the pleas for forgiveness from the sinners. Understood the deep burden of pain their sins created and knew his job was long in coming. He was weary of the endless ways some of them attempted to bargain with God, with life, with death.

But he promised them salvation.

"The truth will set you free," he said quietly.

The woman looked up at him with tear-swollen eyes. Her fingers were red and bloody where she'd tried to claw her way to freedom. Like his last captive, she was a fighter. But she'd made a mistake when she'd forsaken her vows. And she must pay.

He yanked her red hair and shoved her to the stone floor beneath his feet. "You must cleanse yourself, now. Wash away your sins. Only then will you have salvation."

"You're the one who sinned," she snarled. "You're not a sainted man. You're a murderer."

"I am doing God's work," he said, "ridding the world of women like you. Women who cheat on their husbands."

His temper flared then, and he brought the knife down, positioning the blade along the top of her breasts so that it pricked her pale skin. Her eyes widened, but she remained still while he tore the wedding ring from her finger.

She flailed her bound arms and legs in an attempt to escape as he dipped her into the icy pool. She sputtered and spit out water, her body trembling, the chill tightening her nipples into turgid peaks. Water cascaded down her naked torso, droplets clinging to her breasts, trickling down into the red curls at the juncture of her thighs.

His mouth watered. His sex hardened, swelled, throbbed for release. But he had to deny himself. He would not take another man's wife from him, not as his lover.

Not the way the man had stolen his wife from him.

Rage at the humiliation she had caused him built within him. The day he'd found her spread-eagle with another man mounting her. In his bed, no less. His own damn bed! All because of that Internet chat room. That swingers club. She had joined it for the excitement, she had said.

She had deserved to die, to suffer.

Just as this woman did.

She screamed as he drove the knife into her chest.

Chapter Nine

Caitlin's knees knocked as she and Miles drove to the medical examiner's office. When they entered, Agent Brown followed, like a bad storm cloud that wouldn't go away. The receptionist asked them to wait in Mullins's office. Brown paced the small utilitarian room, then turned to Miles, but only after giving her a cold look.

"There's some new information I uncovered, Monahue. I think you should know."

A sense of foreboding overcame her. What had he found out?

"Sit down, Miss Collier," Agent Brown said.

Caitlin sank onto the chair, so weak now she couldn't have stood anyway. Miles shifted and planted one hand on the back of her chair.

"What's going on?" Miles asked.

Agent Brown drummed his knuckles on the table, then flipped a folder open and gestured toward a file. "My agents have done some checking. As I said before, we couldn't find records of a Nora Collier through the DMV or social security office."

"I don't understand," Caitlin said.

"Someone erased all records of your sister's life," Agent Brown said. "Or at least they tried to, but we retrieved them."

Caitlin chewed her lip, her stomach knotting. "But why would they do that?"

"You tell us, Caitlin." Agent Brown leaned back in the chair, the wooden legs squeaking. "You're the one who confiscated your parents' trust fund and placed it in your name. If you had a sister, you obviously didn't want to share the family money with her."

The air whooshed from Caitlin's lungs. "What are you talking about? Let me see that report."

Agent Brown handed her the evidence. "This is called a motive, Miss Collier. Your motive for having your sister killed, then erasing her identity."

MILES CLOSED HIS EYES momentarily to temper his anger. He had no idea Caitlin had had money. Worse, financial gain gave Caitlin a reason to kill her sister, but also added to his motive.

If he had done so and mistaken Nora for her twin, or if the two of them had conspired together...

He took one look at her pale face, though, and his heart squeezed with unwanted emotions. He'd been fighting them ever since she'd walked into his office, and he couldn't help himself now. He wanted to believe her, to defend her.

He hadn't killed her sister, and for some odd reason, he didn't think Caitlin had.

Still, Brown sounded as if he suspected Caitlin of the crime; he probably thought she and this Hollinsby guy might have worked together.

He fisted his hands, and forced himself to focus on Caitlin's behavior. Could he be wrong? Was she such a consummate liar that she continued to fool him with her act of grief?

"I didn't…would not kill my sister," Caitlin said. "She was the only family I had." She stood, rubbed her hands up and down her arms and began to pace. "Nora was my twin, for heaven's sake. My other half. We were as close as two people could get, we shared a special language when we were small. We were inseparable."

"Twins often suffer identity crises when they get older. They argue, fight, compete with one another. Often one harbors a deep-seated jealousy of the look-alike." He paused dramatically. "In rare cases, one suffers psychological problems and that jealousy escalates to violence."

Caitlin staggered back as if she'd been slapped, and Miles stood, ready to do battle for her. "Brown—"

"Let me finish." Agent Brown drummed his knuckles on the table again, and Miles wondered what other revelations he had in that file. "You claim you were held against your will in a psychiatric ward on Nighthawk Island, that Dr. Hollinsby is your doctor, and Tammy Waters said he was having an affair with a patient." His tone was dark. "And now his wife is missing, too. It seems obvious to me that you and Hollinsby are involved."

He stood, propped his hands on the table and pushed his face into Caitlin's. Miles recognized the intimidating stance—he'd used it himself.

"You and Hollinsby either conspired to kill your sister or hired someone to do it so the two of you could be together. A copycat crime. And now you've gotten rid of his wife, too."

Caitlin trembled. "That's ridiculous. I'm terrified of that man—"

"You made the death appear to be a ritualistic murder," Agent Brown continued in a cold voice. "Then you concocted this amnesia story to cover yourselves."

"I wouldn't do such a horrible thing," Caitlin argued. "I loved Nora, I…miss her…."

"Stop lying, Miss Collier. Hollinsby's research is on short- and long-term memory disorders. He also conducted several twin studies and wrote his thesis on twin identity crisis. It was easy for him to help you stage your act."

Mullins knocked on the door, and called Brown out for a minute.

Miles grimaced. He didn't like being in the dark. And Brown's attack had to stop.

Although logically, as a cop, Brown's theory made perfect sense. So, why did he feel as if Caitlin were telling the truth? That she didn't have the mind of a masterful killer, but that she'd been an innocent victim in some diabolical scheme instead?

A scheme he would crack open if it killed him…

CAITLIN FELT NUMB as Agent Brown left. She should be straining her mind to remember the awful things she'd done, and her stay at the psychiatric ward, so she could help find her sister's killer, but her brain and body had completely shut down. She wanted this nightmare to end. She wanted her sister alive. She wanted Miles to believe her, to take her back and forgive her for whatever she'd done.

"Are you all right?"

She glanced up at Miles, surprised to see concern in his eyes.

"How can I be all right?" she asked in a soft whisper. "My sister is gone, the police think I conspired to kill her and everyone insists I'm a horrid person." She chewed her bottom lip. "Even you hate me."

The emotions she'd tried to keep at bay when Agent Brown had questioned her rose to the surface like a tidal wave ready to break free.

"I don't hate you." He must have sensed she'd reached the breaking point, because he touched her arm gently in a comforting gesture, but nausea rose to Caitlin's throat, and she ran toward the bathroom. Inside, she leaned over the sink, tears trickling down her cheeks, her head spinning. She splashed cold water on her face, heaved for air, then stared at her reflection.

Was she the horrible person she'd been portrayed to be? Had she stolen her parents' money and hidden it from Nora? Had she hurt her sister or caused her death?

A ghostlike image of her look-alike's face standing beside her filled the mirror. Her voice whispered from the grave. Old childhood memories rushed back. As if watching from a screen far away, she saw herself and Nora when they were four years old. Santa Claus had left them identical baby dolls for Christmas. Caitlin had loved the baby doll, had named it and fed it with a plastic bottle, had carried it with her everywhere she'd gone and treated it as if it were a real child. Nora had balked at receiving "twin" gifts, had left the doll under the tree, announced that she wanted to be a singer, not a boring mommy. Then she'd fashioned a microphone out of a toilet paper roll and created a show for the family, singing at the top of her lungs.

Even though they had differences in personalities, that

night they'd huddled in bed and whispered and giggled as they'd watched the snowflakes dot their bedroom window.

Another time, when they were ten, their mother had urged them to dress alike for the mother-daughter tea at church. Caitlin had loved the lacy dress that mimicked an adult version of their mother's, but Nora had flatly refused. She'd screamed that she didn't want to be like Caitlin. Caitlin had cried that night, thinking her sister hated her. But once again, Nora had crawled in bed beside her and fabricated wild stories about the adventures the two of them would have when they grew up. Caitlin had hung on to every word, awed at her sister's imagination.

She fast-forwarded to when they were teenagers. Nora had been flirty and outgoing. All the boys had liked her. But in tenth grade, Caitlin had developed a crush on a basketball player. He'd finally asked her for a date, but later she'd learned he'd only asked her to make Nora jealous because he'd really wanted Nora.

Nora had thought it was funny, had belly laughed and offered Caitlin hints on how to seduce boys. But Caitlin had been hurt by Nora's teasing.

There hadn't been any bedtime chat that night or making amends. And they had drifted even further apart over the years.

"Caitlin?" Miles's voice, followed by a knock on the door, broke in to her thoughts. "Are you okay?"

"I'm fine." She patted her face dry, knowing she'd just told a lie. Nothing was fine. And it wouldn't be.

Not ever again.

She glanced in the mirror one more time. She didn't know the woman staring back. Was it possible that she'd hated her sister, that she had conspired to kill her?

MILES COULDN'T HELP HIMSELF. Caitlin had looked so heartbroken and distraught that he slipped into the bathroom. He couldn't make himself believe that she would hurt anyone. Especially her own twin sister.

Her lower lip trembled, and he went to her and took her in his arms. One touch and she leaned into him and whimpered. "I'm sorry, Miles. I…really did love my sister. I swear I did. I don't understand any of this."

But what about him? Had she loved him or simply used him?

He tensed, and started to pull away. But she felt so good, so right, so soft and loving in his arms, that he didn't. What difference did it make now if she had loved him or used him?

She needed help. Maybe mental help. And she definitely needed protection.

Even though he should save himself and walk away, he couldn't.

Instead, he traced a thumb beneath her chin, then lifted her face gently and kissed her. She tasted like sweetness and sin and everything he'd ever wanted or dreamed about having in a woman. Yet even as she melted in his arms, a voice warned him to be cautious.

He shunned the voice and deepened the kiss, his body hot and fiery from the throaty moan she emitted as she melted in his arms.

Suddenly a knock broke the spell he'd fallen under, and Miles slowly pulled away from Caitlin. She looked impossibly pale and small in the dim glow from the bathroom, and fear darkened her eyes.

Then the door swung open and Agent Brown's scrutinizing gaze pinned them with accusations. "Dr. Mullins is ready to talk to us now."

Miles had lost objectivity. Still, he straightened his shoulders and forced his professional mask into place as he guided Caitlin through the door into the hallway. The lights were bald, bright and condemning as they filed back into the medical examiner's office together.

Dr. Mullins was about Miles's age, with thin brown hair cropped short on the top and sides, almost military style. His nose was crooked, as if it had once been broken, his body lean and fit, his demeanor solemn. Miles couldn't imagine the strength it took to do his job.

In spite of the strong cleaning chemicals, the metallic scent of blood, and the stench of human body parts and death permeated the building. Caitlin inhaled a calming breath herself, the tremble of her lower lip a definite sign of nerves.

"You have some information for us?" Agent Brown said.

"Yes." Mullins removed his rubber gloves and gestured toward the file on his desk while Miles, Caitlin and Brown claimed seats in the vinyl chairs facing him. "I thought you might want to hear this in person."

"What did you find?" Miles asked.

"Judging from the bruising, dehydration and other details, the victim was abducted about three weeks ago." Mullins glanced at Caitlin, then back at Miles. "As far as cause of death, the victim bled out from the stab wounds. The knife punctured the chest, went right through the aorta. Death was quick."

Miles heard the part he omitted. Death was quick, *but not painless.*

"She sustained other injuries during her captivity,

minor bruising to the chest, abominable area, her hands and arms. But there was no sign of rape."

"DNA?" Agent Brown asked.

"None." He shook his head, thumbing through the pages of the report. "He used a cleaning solution to clean the victim, most likely before he killed her."

Miles ground his jaw. Beside him Caitlin flinched, holding on to the chair edge as if to steady herself.

"There's something else you'll find interesting." Once again, he leveled his gaze on Caitlin. "We ran the DNA samples you gave us, Miss Collier, and I managed to locate dental records from you and your sister."

"What did you find?" Miles asked, unable to stand the tension.

"The woman on the table is not Nora Collier." Mullins steepled his hands, then hissed an exaggerated breath. "She's Caitlin."

Miles's pulse clamored.

Agent Brown slid forward to examine the findings. "Are you certain?"

"Yes. I managed to locate medical records on the Collier twins when they were children." He gestured toward the woman beside Miles. "Nora had an emergency appendectomy when she was six. Caitlin didn't. There is no scar on the dead woman or evidence of surgery."

Miles stared at the woman he'd thought was Caitlin. She shrank in the chair, a bewildered look pulling at her face. Miles struggled to remember the night she'd shown up at his door when he'd undressed her and tucked her into bed, but he hadn't noticed the details of her body that night, at least not a scar. He'd been too shell-shocked to pay attention. And then when he'd kissed her and stripped that shirt, he'd been too fired up from wanting her to notice. But Mullins was right—he hadn't seen a scar on Caitlin. Or the woman he'd thought was Caitlin...

"You want to check it?" Agent Brown cut in.

She jerked her head up, trembling. When her eyes met Miles's, he read a mixture of emotions. Confusion, fear, denial. Yet she had showered and undressed herself and had to know.

"Let's see for sure," Miles hissed.

She bit her lip, her hands shaking as she slowly unfastened her jeans and slid the material down a fraction of an inch, then lower.

"The scar would have faded," Mullins said. "But you should still be able to detect the faint outline of the surgical procedure."

Miles saw it then. The thin surgical scar was so faint he might not have noticed, but the skin was slightly discolored.

This woman wasn't his wife, as she'd claimed, but his wife's sister.

Jesus. And he had almost fallen for her. Almost made love to her. Almost believed her...

But why had she lied about her identity? What kind of twisted game was she playing? Or was she really delusional, as Dr. Gailstorm had suggested?

"There's something else you should know," Mullins said in a low voice.

Miles's mouth thinned into a straight line. God, what else could there be?

"What is it?" Agent Brown asked, giving Caitlin—no, Nora—a skeptical look.

"Your victim, Caitlin Collier Monahue, was pregnant."

Miles rocked back in his chair, his head roaring as if

someone had slammed him with a brick. Beside him, Nora gasped, then hugged her arms around herself as if she, too, had been punched.

"Pregnant?" The gruff voice came from Miles, although he barely recognized it.

"Yes." Mullins folded his arms across the desk. "A few weeks at least."

Miles cleared his throat. An image of him and Caitlin together, making love, robbed his lungs of air. The family he'd never had, the one he'd dreamt about when he'd been all alone after his parents' murder, had been within his grasp.

But Caitlin's deceptions filtered through the haze. Had the baby been his? And if so, why hadn't she told him he was going to be a father?

And why was her sister here now pretending to be her? Had she killed his wife and baby, copied The Carver's MO, then returned to collect the family money? Or was she worried that he would receive it, so she'd decided to pretend to be his wife to seduce it out of him?

Chapter Ten

Nora clenched her hands in her lap, her head spinning. What was going on? Why had she believed she was Caitlin if she was Nora? Sure, she'd experienced a few odd moments where she'd doubted her identity, but she had memories of being Caitlin. Memories of Caitlin's feelings toward *her.*

Although she hadn't remembered Miles…because she'd never met him.

But her dream about Miles had been so real.

Anger and betrayal darkened his eyes. Disappointment flared there, too, as if he hadn't known about the baby.

She wanted to comfort him, assure him that she didn't understand why her sister would have betrayed him, that she was sorry his child was gone. Caitlin must have been desperate. But her desperation didn't warrant using a man like Miles….

A man like Miles. A man who'd wanted Caitlin. Who'd been seduced by her sultry voice and sweetness. A man who loved her sister.

The growing attraction *she'd* experienced since being with him could never go anywhere, because he didn't want her, Nora—he wanted her sister, just as all the other men in her life had.

Guilt erupted through the haze of confusion, too. How selfish was she? How could she even contemplate wanting Miles when her sister was dead? When he was looking at her with suspicion?

She'd have to find someplace else to stay. She couldn't return to his house and sleep in the bed he'd once shared with Caitlin, the bed where they'd made a baby....

Not with the man who thought she'd killed his wife and child.

A DEAFENING SILENCE lingered in the room as Miles processed this latest revelation, but he knew the question had to be asked. If he didn't, Brown would.

He braced his elbows on his knees, his head clenched between his hands. "Do you have any idea who the father was?"

"Not exactly," Mullins said.

"What does that mean?" Agent Brown asked.

"I can tell you who it's not."

"It wasn't mine," Miles said in a deadpan voice.

"No." Mullins hesitated. "I did some tests. Preliminary bloodwork rules you out."

Miles nodded, the truth sinking in. He'd wondered why Caitlin had been so eager to run to the Justice of the Peace. Now he knew. She was looking for a father for her baby. Only she hadn't bothered to inform him.

How could he have been so gullible?

"So now, the charges might be upped to a double homicide?" Agent Brown asked. "You want to tell us why you lied about your identity, Miss Collier?"

"I…I didn't. I thought I was Caitlin." Her voice caught. "They must have scrambled my memories in that psychiatric unit to convince me I was my sister."

Her excuse sounded too bizarre to be believed.

Miles stood, his hands fisted by his sides. The pregnancy stamped another motive onto the growing list of reasons to have wanted his wife dead. If he were standing in Brown's shoes, he might already have slapped the handcuffs around his wrists.

Of course, knowing that it was Nora who was alive and not Caitlin, that Caitlin had cheated her sister out of her inheritance, also painted suspicion on Nora.

Had she erased records of her own identity? If so, why? So she could assume Caitlin's identity to gain access to the inheritance? Had she shown up at his door pretending to be her sister, trying to win him over, so he would help her?

The heated kiss they'd shared rushed back to haunt him. In his gut, he'd sensed something was different. Oh, the kiss had been passionate and filled with hunger just as it had been with Caitlin at first, but there had been something different, something he couldn't put his finger on. A desperation born of lies? Had Nora been trying to lure him into her bed as Caitlin had?

Was she just as manipulative as her sister?

And what did the twins' identities have to do with The Carver?

NORA STRUGGLED to sort out her feelings, as well as her memories, as she and Miles left the medical examiner's office. He pushed his shades on, silent, brooding, obviously contemplating the fact that his wife was dead and *she* was alive.

No doubt he would have rather it been her in the morgue than Caitlin.

And that poor baby.

Caitlin's child, her niece or nephew, was gone as well.

Grief welled inside her. Who was the father? If they knew the answer, would it lead them to Caitlin's killer?

And why had she thought *she* was Caitlin?

She closed her eyes, forcing herself to recall the details she'd learned so far about her past. She'd met her sister in that bar….

A gray curtain dropped over the rest of the evening. The baby…something about the baby triggered a faint memory. She and her sister discussing a child…

She pressed her fingers to her temple. *Go over it again.*

She'd met Caitlin—had they talked? Shared secrets? Had Caitlin confided about Miles and her marriage, and the baby?

Miles…her heart squeezed, sympathy for him warring with her own budding need. She'd been dependent on him for days, had burrowed in his home and been comforted by his strength.

It was time to stop.

But she still needed answers. Maybe she'd witnessed Caitlin's kidnapping and had suffered a breakdown. But if so, why had Dr. Hollinsby refused to acknowledge he'd treated her?

The nightmares of her own screams from inside the place echoed in her mind. The dizziness from the drugs… Had Dr. Hollinsby killed Caitlin? If they'd had an affair, could Caitlin's baby be Dr. Hollinsby's child? Had he killed her to keep his wife from finding out?

If so, then why kill his wife? Unless she'd discovered

his affair. But why put *her* in the hospital and drug her? So she'd forget...

They reached the town, and she scanned the streets. On first appearance, Raven's Peak seemed quaint. Even beautiful. But a killer roamed the streets. Caitlin's killer? Was he here in town? Hiding out in the mountains?

Miles's expression remained tight-lipped. The ride back to his cabin was tense and quiet. When they entered, he built a fire, then grabbed a beer from the refrigerator and booted up his computer.

"Miles, what if Dr. Hollinsby fathered Caitlin's baby?"

He paused and shot her a cold look. "I've already considered the possibility. It would definitely give him motive for murder." He twisted his mouth sideways, and she sensed deep pain within him. "It might also explain his missing wife."

"Maybe she left him when she found out he had an affair," Nora suggested. "Or perhaps she confronted him and then he killed her."

"It's possible." His dark eyes assessed her. "You're really Caitlin's twin then?" he asked in a gruff voice. "And you didn't know?"

"I must be Nora, but I'm confused. I've had Caitlin's memories, and some of Nora's. How is that possible?" Unless she really had needed psychiatric care.

"You suspected and said nothing?"

"I didn't know what to believe." She shoved a hand through her hair. "I swear, Miles, I'm telling the truth. How about you? Didn't you know the difference?"

His mouth flattened into a thin line, the memory of the kiss surfacing. Could he differentiate his wife's kiss from her sister's?

"I wondered," he said quietly, letting the comment sink into the charged air radiating between them. Finally he cleared his throat. "Did you know about the baby?"

She frowned and moved up to the fire, warming her hands. That nagging sensation plucked at her again, and she looked at the fish in the tank. She had recognized them immediately. But Nora would have known that Caitlin had fish….

"Did you know?" Miles asked, his voice harder.

She fidgeted with her hands. "No. I…maybe she told me that night we met at the bar, but I can't recall the details of our conversation."

Suspicion clouded his face. This man had been burned so badly he'd never believe her, no matter what she said.

Firelight glinted off his black hair, the only light glimmering in the dark room. He seemed to prefer the shadows. And those Ray-Bans he wore—was he trying to hide behind them, shield his emotions?

Still, she felt drawn to him, so compelled that it was difficult for her to speak, so she walked to the closet in search of a bag to pack her belongings.

"What are you doing?" he asked in a gruff voice.

"Looking for a suitcase. I have to leave."

One thick eyebrow shot up, the only sign of a reaction to her announcement. His big hands were folded, his breathing even, his long legs stretched in front of him as he studied her.

"Why?"

"There's no reason for me to stay here any longer."

"So, you're running?"

She heard the silent implications. *Because the cops are on to you.*

"I don't belong here, Miles," she said in a strained

whisper. In fact, she didn't belong anywhere. Not anymore.

He didn't argue. "Did Caitlin tell you who fathered her child?"

Her heart squeezed for him. "No. I…wish she had, Miles. I wish I could help, but I've told you the truth. I don't know what else to say."

Except that she thought she was falling in love with him. In spite of everything—the drugs, the confusion, her lost memories, the ones tangled with Caitlin's—she wanted to be with him.

Yet he had loved her sister.

He stood, his chair hitting the floor with a whack. "It's too dangerous for you to leave now, Nora."

But it was too dangerous for her to stay here. She'd end up wanting him more, making a fool out of herself. "I'll be fine," she said. "If you don't want to drive me to a motel, I can call a taxi."

A muscle ticked in his jaw as he stalked toward her. "Not tonight. I told you it's not safe," he said, biting out the words. "Besides, we're going to Nighthawk Island tomorrow and find out what happened there."

A shudder rippled through her, but she reluctantly agreed, then huddled by the fire. Revisiting that hospital terrified her, but if it would help her piece together the truth about what had happened to her and Caitlin, she had to go. She'd just have to keep her distance from Miles until they returned.

MILES HAD SCHOOLED his reaction to Nora's announcement, but the idea of her leaving had totally rattled him. It was too dangerous for her. The killer might come after her, might be watching for a time when she was alone so he could strike. And Hollinsby was still missing.

But a nagging voice whispered that wasn't the real reason he didn't want her to leave. He liked having her here. Liked her sleeping in his bed.

God, he was a twisted bastard.

Angry at himself, he turned to the computer and lost himself in researching Hollinsby and CIRP, the Coastal Island Research Park, in Savannah.

He didn't think that Nora had conspired with Hollinsby or anyone else to kill Caitlin. Most serial killers worked alone.

But not all. And if it were a copycat crime…

Curious about twin studies, and Hollinsby's work, he downloaded several articles and skimmed them. Some twin studies focused on the similarities between twins, the psychic connection, the chemical and physical qualities. Others reported cases in which twins had been raised separately, in completely different environments, yet they had chosen almost identical career paths and hobbies, and shared similarities in spousal choice. In several studies, they had given their children the same names without realizing it.

Other studies focused on the differences, the difficulties of being a twin, the sibling rivalry, jealousy, competitiveness. Some twins had a love/hate relationship with their look-alike, some were complete opposites in personalities. In a few cases, one twin had actually tried to destroy or kill the other so he/she could have his/her own identity. Often, in the adolescent stage, twins who had been close as young children split, and began to have problems as they struggled to establish their own unique identity.

He read on, skimmed an article about the death of one twin. The surviving one often suffered survivor guilt, felt as if a part of themselves had died.

Some identical twins could read each other's thoughts. They were even known to experience the other's feelings, their pain and emotions.

Hmm. A half dozen scenarios raced through his head. Maybe Nora had felt Caitlin's fear or pain when she was kidnapped and had wound up in the mental ward seeking help. Maybe she invented the story about the psychiatric ward to use an insanity defense if arrested.

He remembered the terror in her eyes and voice when she'd first arrived, and dismissed the idea. She had been scared. Hurt. Ill. And she was grief-stricken now.

He consulted the files on Hollinsby again. Hubert Hollinsby grew up in a strict Baptist home in rural North Georgia. Born to Henrietta and Larry Hollinsby. His mother died when the boy was thirteen. His father was a preacher, but he'd died two years before.

Brown punched in the number of the Savannah Police Department, and asked to speak to Adam Black, a detective who had been quoted in several articles regarding Nighthawk Island. He explained the case and listened while Black filled him in on the shady cases he'd related to the research park.

"We have inside sources undercover on Nighthawk Island," Black said.

"I need to know if Dr. Hubert Hollinsby worked on a project there. He's a psychiatrist."

Black put him on hold, and Miles accessed all the articles he could on Nighthawk Island and CIRP while he waited. Seconds later, Black returned to the line.

"Yes. Hollinsby was in Savannah for the last year, but he recently transferred to another research park. A new one that's just opened up."

"Here in Raven's Peak."

"That's it," Detective Black said.

Dammit. It was too coincidental. He had to investigate Nora Collier's story and see if there was an ounce of truth to it. If Hollinsby had had an affair with Caitlin, and Nora discovered it, perhaps he'd admitted her to the mental ward to keep her from talking.

But if he was their killer, why hadn't he murdered Nora as well?

And if he'd killed Caitlin, was her murder a copycat crime or was he the serial killer stalking the South?

DR. ARTHUR MULLINS contemplated Sheriff Monahue's reaction to the information he'd given him. Was the man surprised to learn the woman with him was Nora Collier instead of his wife? Was he sleeping with her?

The two women were as identical as any twins he'd ever seen. DNA, forensic science, the corpses—he'd always found them fascinating.

Science never lied.

Not like women.

He gave a sarcastic laugh, then turned and strode back to the cold room where another woman's dead body waited. Two doors, one marked Body Receiving, the other Body Pick-up. They also had a special room for the doctors to extract the donor's organs.

He opened the door to Body Receiving and stepped in to the frigid room, then glanced at the woman lying on the steel slab. He unzipped the body bag. She was wide-eyed, pale, the veins under her skin blue beneath the bright light. He patted her stiff, cold hand. She hadn't been gone long. Still had that look of shock etched on her face as if she couldn't believe that death had come for her. Poor thing. So young.

Another smile curved his lips. His hands itched to touch her.

Her family would want answers.

Time for him to do his job. Do what he did best.

Carve her up and tell them how she had died.

Chapter Eleven

Nora found blankets and an extra pillow in Miles's closet and spread them on the couch. She had no right to sleep in his bed, to want him to hold her, to lust after her sister's husband. Grief consumed her, the thought of returning to Nighthawk Island sending a tremor through her.

"What are you doing?"

Miles moved away from the computer and massaged his neck. His gaze slid over her, then back to her eyes, and a muscle ticked in his jaw. She'd changed into that damn nightshirt again, and he wished she had flannel pajamas instead.

"I'm sleeping out here tonight, Miles. I don't expect you to give up your bed for me." Although she desperately wanted to share it with him.

What kind of woman did that make her? She'd take her sister's leftovers, let him pretend she was Caitlin if he wanted....

No, she might not have all her memories intact, but she did have pride.

He shook his head. "Take the bed, Nora. I doubt I'll sleep tonight, anyway."

"But, Miles—"

"Don't argue with me," he snapped. "I intend to study up on that research park. I want to be armed with knowledge when we approach them tomorrow."

"You do believe I was held there?" she said, aching for his trust.

"I…don't know what to believe anymore."

Emotions clogged her throat. She'd never felt so alone in all her life. And she couldn't blame Miles for holding back. She was the troubled sister of the woman he'd loved, a woman who looked like his dead wife who had deceived him and died carrying another man's child. He probably hated them both, wished he'd never met them.

"I'm sorry," she said, her voice warbling. "I…as soon as we learn what happened to Caitlin, I'll get out of your life."

He worked his mouth from side to side, as if he wanted to say something, but then his eyes darkened with anguish, and he refrained from speaking. She turned and rushed into the bedroom before she collapsed into tears and begged him to love her, at least for the night.

Drained, and exhausted from the day's ordeal, she stretched out on the bed. Miles's scent enveloped her, the imprint of his big, hard, strong body had left an impression on the bedding. She rolled to her side and pulled her knees to her chest, then hugged his pillow to her, inhaling his masculine odor and praying for the strength to leave him when the time came for her to do so.

But where would she go?

She had no money…except for her parents' inheritance, and that would be tied up until all doubts were erased concerning her sister's death. She had no ID. No home. She'd have to find a job. What had she done for a living? She remembered singing in that bar, but somehow she couldn't imagine returning to that lifestyle. The thought of performing on stage, of having strange men gawking at her, sent a shiver of apprehension up her spine.

But what else could she do? What skills did she possess?

Her head was throbbing, so she closed her eyes, willing herself to forget the grueling interrogation by the federal agent and Miles's condemning stare. Her sister's image flashed into the darkness again, though. The ghostlike whisper of her voice echoed around her, pleading with her to find her killer.

Tears clogged her throat. She should have died instead of her sister. Then she wouldn't be here all alone.

Finally exhaustion overcame her, and she drifted into a fitful sleep. But nightmares haunted her, bombarding her with pictures of the past.

First, she was a child, and she and her sister were fighting.

"Why can't you be like your sister, Caitlin?" her mother scolded. "She's such a sweet, docile child. She never causes any trouble."

"She's afraid of her own shadow."

"She loves you, Nora. You're twins, you should love her, too."

"I'm not the good twin's clone," Nora shouted. "I don't want to be like her!"

Then she was older, still fighting for attention, still sharing it with the good twin.

More dreams invaded her sleep as if she had turned back the clock. She was dressed in a black slinky dress with red stiletto heels. Her hair lay in loose waves, swaying around her shoulders as she walked across a stage. She arched her back, thrusting her breasts upward, her gaze glued to the dark-haired enigmatic stranger in the back. The minute she met his gaze, heat exploded between them. Her nipples tightened to hard peaks as his gaze drifted over her body. She arched her back even farther, begging him to see the needy hunger beneath the silk-clad package. Her voice crooned out, floating in the smoky air between them, and he moved closer, his lips quirked into a cocky, come-get-me smile as he parked himself in the chair in front of the stage.

She danced around him, singing softly, letting her hips sway to the seductive tune, savoring the fiery tension between them. This man wanted her for herself. Not for her sister.

He turned up his beer bottle and drank slowly, his lips closing around the end of the bottle as if closing around her breasts. She could almost hear him sucking, feel him licking her skin. It was on fire, hot need burning inside her and begging for release. She smiled, watching his throat muscles work, wondering how any man could be so damn sexy with his clothes on and not having even touched her.

But there was something about those eyes, uncovered, naked, yearning. They were so dark, mysterious, penetrating deep into her soul. They drew her, held a wicked power that made her desperate for the raw passion beneath his rigidly controlled movements.

She trailed her fingers down her arms in an erotic game, her movements across the stage mimicking the teasing of a lover's caress as she imagined his lips tracing a path where her own fingers teased.

Then he'd held out his hand, and they'd danced until dawn. And later, he'd led her to his bed. He stripped his clothes in the moonlight, then stood naked and proud before her. The subtle play of shadows across bronzed muscles painted a portrait of male beauty, but it was his hard sex pulsing against the dark hair on his thighs that took her breath away. She had never wanted a man like this.

Had never felt as if the world might explode if she didn't welcome him inside her body and let him take her for a ride.

Moisture pooled between her legs, the heavy ache of her breasts was almost painful as he inched the spaghetti straps of her dress down her shoulders. And when his lips brushed her skin, fire ignited in a stormy path over her body, sending shards of pleasure rippling through her. Then he spread her on the bed, licked, tasted and teased every inch of her, and she opened for him, begging for the pleasure that only he could offer.

And when he thrust inside her, his throaty groan of release triggering her own, she knew she wasn't alone anymore. She had found her lover. Her soul mate.

Nora jerked awake, her breathing ragged, sweat trickling down her skin, her body hot and shaking. What had just happened?

She'd been dreaming she was making love with Miles. In his arms, she had felt his need, his hunger, and she'd been whole.

But it was only a dream, and now she felt empty inside.

The sound of the computer keys clicking in the background indicated he hadn't come to bed. That the reality of her lies still stood between them. That the well of emptiness inside her ran deep.

But the feel of his lips on her skin still tingled.

Had she been dreaming or had the sexual interlude

been a memory returning to haunt her with a reminder of everything she'd lost?

But how could she remember being with him if she had never slept with the man?

THE FIRE CRACKLED and popped in the silence. Night came and went as Miles accessed every available source he could find on the Internet, and studied the history of the research park and the experimental work being conducted. The research spanned every imaginable bioengineering project and topic possible. Of course, the CIRP boasted of cutting-edge techniques and research, government funding, and top-notch scientists and doctors.

But Detective Black had e-mailed him information from his files that detailed secret projects gone awry, scientists being killed to cover up secrets, shady experiments conducted to erase a cop's memory when he uncovered unethical work, and even a project that had used children for genetic engineering and brainwashed them into being spies.

He glanced back at his bedroom where Nora Collier slept. After reading Black's files, her story didn't sound so bizarre. Agent Brown suspected her of working with Hollinsby to hurt her sister. What if it was the other way around? What if she'd stumbled onto their affair or witnessed her sister's kidnapping and had a breakdown, or Hollinsby had drugged her to keep her from telling his wife? Trauma could cause amnesia.

Then Nora had been a victim, just as her sister...

His body jerked in response, the urge to go to her eating at him. The urge to hold her was even stronger. She was in his bed. Sleeping. Vulnerable. Alone.

But she was not his wife. She never had been. Yet he

had brought her into his home, had held her and kissed her, had wanted her as if she was.

Because she looked exactly like her sister? Or had he somehow known all along that they were different?

He scrubbed his hand over his face, stretched out on the sofa in his jeans and closed his eyes, trying like hell not to answer that question. He had to forget he'd ever touched her. Yet, an image of her in those damn panties floated back, her pale creamy throat begging for a taste, her nipples distended as if they needed a man's mouth, *his* mouth, her eyes imploring him to take her.

He punched the pillow and rolled to his side, willing himself to forget that kiss ever happened. To remind himself that she'd asked to leave tonight, that tomorrow he'd drive her to Nighthawk Island and hopefully get to the bottom of this puzzle. Then he'd find Caitlin's killer.

And what if taking Nora back to that island placed her in imminent danger?

Anxiety drove him off the couch to pace for another hour, his emotions riding a roller coaster. Part of him hated her, didn't trust her, suspected she was manipulative like her sister.

Another part knew she wasn't. Her touch, her eyes, the anguish and vulnerability…the simmering emotions below the passion—they were different.

But she shared the same face as his dead wife.

Caitlin. She'd lied to him, cheated on him, married him to give her baby a father and not even told him. Then she'd decided even a baby wasn't worth staying together for.

And what would he have done if he'd known she was pregnant?

God, when he was little and his parents had been

murdered, he'd wanted a family so badly, he used to imagine his folks coming back at Christmas. Would he have tried to make a family work with her and her unborn child?

How about Nora? Had she shown up on his doorstep playing an innocent, traumatized victim so she could seduce him into trusting her? Then would she take her parents' money and run? Or was she a victim, too?

He dropped his head into his hands and groaned in frustration.

Finally, he hit the couch again. He'd be no good the next day if he didn't at least close his eyes for a second. Sometime later, he fell into a fitful sleep.

But he dreamt of Caitlin, and Nora, look-alikes he couldn't tell apart.

And a little baby who was crying for him, one who looked like his wife. An infant he wanted to call his own, one he'd lost before it was even born.

NORA WOKE AT DAWN, the nightmares from the evening before plucking at her nerves. Daylight brought reality crashing back like a bad train wreck knocking off casualties in its wake.

Today she had to return to Nighthawk Island. To a place that had kept her captive, a place that had stolen her memories and weeks of her life, a place she'd escaped physically but one that haunted her day and night.

Anger fortified her as she showered and dressed. Grief and guilt compounded her emotions, making her well aware of Miles's anguish over the revelations from the day before as she entered the kitchen and poured herself a cup of coffee.

Thirty minutes later, Miles's silence reeked of betrayal

as they drove toward Savannah. The six-hour drive was strained and quiet, unanswered questions lingering between them. He seemed so tense that she ached to reach out and comfort him, to soothe his pain. To let him know that they could mourn Caitlin together. If only she understood her twin's actions.

Why had her sister cheated on Miles with another man? And why had she married him if she didn't love him? Who was the father of her baby? It wasn't like Caitlin to sleep around.

She gripped her hands together, frowning.

Caitlin…she had always been the *good* twin. The quieter one, the one her parents gushed over because she didn't talk back. Caitlin had never slept around, had been loyal, a friend until the end.

Nora had been obstinate, stubborn—the fun, outgoing girl, a flirt. She liked men.

Had Caitlin loved Miles? If so, why hadn't *she* attended the wedding? Caitlin would have been excited over getting married, would have invited her. Would have wanted her twin at the ceremony. Would have meant her vows.

Unless she needed a father for her baby and she was desperate.

Had someone hurt her sister, maybe raped her and gotten her pregnant, then abandoned her? Had Caitlin been so desperate to give her unborn baby a father that she'd turned to a stranger, and tricked Miles into marriage?

A nagging little voice seeped into her head—if Caitlin hadn't loved Miles, then why couldn't she and he be together?

Because *he* had loved Caitlin.

By early afternoon, they sat in Dr. Ian Hall's office. He

offered a brief history of CIRP, the Coastal Island Research Park, and boasted about the cutting-edge work and scientists on staff.

"Let me reassure you that since I've assumed leadership of this facility, we've experienced no problems. We top the United States in medical research and bioengineering, and have a half dozen government-funded projects underway at this time. You'll be seeing great things from our researchers over the next year." He paused and indicated a plaque on the wall. "In fact, we're now part of the Georgia Research Alliance, and have established a special commission to work in association with the governor himself."

Miles steepled his hands and explained about the serial killer in Raven's Peak.

"I don't understand what that has to do with CIRP," Dr. Hall said.

"This killer murdered three victims in Savannah, then two in Atlanta, starting nine months ago. Miss Collier's twin sister, Caitlin, was a victim of The Carver," Miles said. "And Miss Collier, Nora, claims she was a patient at the Nighthawk Island center, that she was restrained in a psychiatric ward by one of your former psychiatrists, Hubert Hollinsby."

Dr. Hall gasped, then skated his eyes over her. "Miss Collier, I'm sorry for your loss, but I don't understand your accusations." He clicked a few keys on his computer and frowned. "I have complete files at my disposal. And your name is not listed anywhere in the system."

"Computer files can be erased or altered," Miles said, then stood. "And I think Nora is telling the truth. Dr. Hollinsby recently transferred to a new facility near us, Black

Mountain Research Hospital. His wife is missing, and now he's missing, as well."

Dr. Hall rocked back in his chair. "You think that Dr. Hollinsby had something to do with his wife's death? That he might be this serial killer?"

"We aren't certain yet. But he is wanted for questioning." Miles leveled his tone. "Now I'd like clearance to go to Nighthawk Island and question the staff in the psychiatric ward."

"I'm afraid that's not possible. Our utmost confidential projects are housed on the island."

"Exactly," Miles said. "And I want to know why *Miss Collier* was part of a confidential project, and what they did to her while she was there."

MILES STUDIED Ian Hall's stony demeanor as he escorted them out of his office. The man hadn't appreciated Miles's threats.

And he *had* threatened him, told him he'd call every reporter in the Southeast and relay Nora's story if he didn't allow him access to the Nighthawk Island facility. The man had still refused, claiming they needed government clearance, which would take weeks, maybe months.

Furious and determined to discover if Nora's story had credence, Miles commandeered a small motorboat, ushered Nora onto it, then headed toward the remote island. The water was choppy, the motor cutting through the water, the small boat bouncing up and down with the blunt force of the winds and crashing waves. Nora huddled inside her jacket, looking jittery and terrified. He wanted to wrap his arms around her and protect her, to assure her that nothing bad would happen to her.

But he couldn't lie. He hadn't been able to protect her sister, his own damned wife—what good would his promises be?

Winter whistled its impending arrival as he shut off the engine and paddled them to an inlet that seemed obscure from the highly monitored security system. Regardless of his caution, though, seconds after they'd climbed ashore, a bevy of semiautomatics and automatics were aimed at their chests.

"We have intruders," one of the military men stated into his radio. He gestured toward Miles. "Identify yourself."

Miles gave his name, flashed his badge and explained that he'd just come from Dr. Ian Hall's office. He tried to send Nora a reassuring look while the man radioed, then spoke to the director of CIRP. Seconds later, the guard commandeered his weapon, then motioned for them to get in to the jeep. Five minutes later, they were seated in an office in the main building on Nighthawk Island.

Armed guards stood at the doorway, keeping them prisoners, as they waited silently for their fate. Nora shivered and hugged her arms around her waist. Was she reliving the weeks she'd spent locked on the island? And how in the hell had she escaped?

Maybe she's telling the truth...

Maybe you're falling in love with her all over again.

No, this woman is not Caitlin—she's her look-alike. A twin you'd never met before Caitlin's death. And how sick are you that you want to be with a woman who is identical to your dead wife?

Even if she were telling the truth, and Hollinsby had kept her here, what did a twin study have to do with The Carver? None of it made sense....

NORA GLANCED AROUND the hallway, the windows and the office, tiny tremors of anxiety rippling through her. The building appeared eerily quiet. But it wasn't silent in the corridors where the patients were restrained. There, screams of terror, the pain of a mind that had been lost or thrust into another world, remained.

But she had survived. And she would not let anyone destroy her.

A tall, angular woman with gaunt features and wiry brown hair strode in, her scowl of disapproval obvious.

"I'm Dr. Livingston. I've been informed of your reasons for being here, and I've checked into the matter myself."

"We want to know who admitted Miss Collier into the facility," Miles announced in a voice that indicated he meant business.

Dr. Livingston glared at him over thick dark glasses. "We have no record of anyone named Collier or Monahue being admitted to the facility." She gestured toward the guards. "Now, it's time for you to leave."

"Please…" Nora stood, her voice imploring. "I'm not crazy. I was here, I know I was. I remember my nurse, a woman named Donna—"

"Maybe you need to see a therapist, Miss Collier," Dr. Livingston said. "Because it sounds to me like you're delusional."

"I'm not delusional," Nora argued. "I remember being here. I remember Donna. I heard nurses talking about the special nighthawk the island is named after, that some-times it preys on humans as well as animals." Her voice rose with conviction. "I even saw one the night I escaped."

"The legend of the nighthawk is public record, Miss

Collier. Anyone could have read about it in the papers or online. I think they're even making small souvenirs of the nighthawk and selling them in Savannah at the gift shops."

Miles cleared his throat. "Check your nursing staff—do you have a nurse named Donna?"

The woman sighed impatiently. "We have at least three Donnas on staff in varying capacities, but I can assure you none of them imprisoned Miss Collier here against her will."

"Tell us about Dr. Hollinsby's projects," Miles snapped. "Was he conducting a twin research study?"

"I'm not at liberty to discuss his work." Dr. Livingston gestured toward the guard again. "Now, I really have business to attend to."

Nora bit down on her lip, reeling with anger as the guards approached them and escorted them across the island and onto the boat.

Miles shot the guards a cold look as he climbed into the driver's seat and started the boat's engine. But at least they returned his weapon. Nora hugged her coat around her as they fought the choppy waters and departed. When they reached the shore on Catcall Island, Miles ushered her into his car and cranked up the heater.

"I can't believe the way they treated us," Nora said. "They wouldn't even let us talk to the staff."

"They're hiding something," he agreed. "And before it's over, Nora, I'll find out what it is. I promise."

Nora wanted to believe him. But after talking to that doctor, doubts assaulted her. One minute she had memories of being Nora, the next, memories that seemed like Caitlin's.

What if she *had* suffered a breakdown? Maybe she was unstable....

MILES GRITTED HIS TEETH as he neared the Savannah police station. Something sinister had happened to Nora on Nighthawk Island. The doctors, staff, guards were all too secretive and protective of their work to convince him they weren't hiding something.

"Let's go inside and talk to Detective Black." Miles gestured toward the building. "He and his partner, Clayton Fox, have been investigating Nighthawk Island for months."

Nora nodded, and followed him inside the local police station. The hum of computers, phones and cops filled the precinct. They sipped stale coffee while the officers relayed information from prior cases associated with the research park.

"After they tried to kill me, they performed plastic surgery on me," Detective Clayton Fox explained. "Then they transplanted memories into my head to make me believe I was another person. And it almost worked."

Nora gaped at him in stunned silence. "I've been having memories of being Nora one minute, and Caitlin the next."

Miles frowned, flexing his fingers in front of him. "Do you think they performed some kind of memory transplant experiment on her?"

Detective Black paced the office. "It's possible. The latest project we uncovered was called SHIP. A group of women were trained, brainwashed, to be spies when they were children. Special Agent Luke Devlin married one of them and broke the project wide open."

"What can we do?" Miles asked. "How do we find out exactly what they did to Nora?"

"Let me talk to our inside contact," Detective Fox said. "Agent Devlin's friend is undercover at the island. Maybe he can help find the answers we need."

DR. OMAR WHITE punched in numbers on his cell phone, sweat beading his forehead as the line rang. Finally the answering machine clicked on and he cursed. "Hollinsby, this is an unbelievable mess. The Collier woman and that sheriff showed up at the center today asking questions. We have to do something. They even managed to sneak onto Nighthawk Island."

The machine bleeped, and he slammed down the phone, then tossed back the drink in his hand, grateful for the slow burn of alcohol. Hollinsby should never have gotten involved with those twins. But he had to accept blame himself.

He should have known that Hollinsby would make a mess of things. The man was too damn emotional. The fool had even joined that secret society of swingers. He wished the man had never shown him that Web site. Wished Hollinsby had never joined it.

Wished he hadn't, either. But it was too late. They were both hooked.

And now the twin project was about to come back and haunt them. That damn sheriff was nosing in, trying to connect them to this crazy serial killer.

He poured himself another drink, then picked up the phone and punched in another number, this one reserved for special circumstances. An old buddy from the military who owed him a favor.

A sniper who never missed his mark and always walked away as if he were invisible.

God help him, he'd have to go attend confession again. Say a million Hail Mary's. Beg the Father to forgive him.

But he had to keep his secrets safe.

Chapter Twelve

Miles checked in with his deputy to make certain things were calm in Raven's Peak, then phoned Agent Brown to see if there were any new developments in The Carver case. He hung up, weary and frustrated. Nothing so far. And the visit to Nighthawk Island had only raised more questions.

But he believed Nora had been detained, and somebody wanted to keep her hospitalization quiet, which only made their motives look suspicious and confirmed that Nora might be telling the truth. They had to find Hollinsby.

"What should we do now?" Nora asked as they left the Savannah Police Department.

"Detective Black will let us know if he or Agent Devlin uncover anything." He scrubbed a hand over the back of his neck. "We need to make funeral arrangements for Caitlin tomorrow."

Nora nodded, pain flashing in her eyes. A pain he felt deep in his soul, as well.

He barely resisted giving her a hug, but climbed into the SUV. "Let's get a hotel here for the night, then get up early and drive back."

She nodded, rubbing her hands together to warm them. He found a motel on the outskirts of Savannah and parked. Maybe it would do them both good to get some rest, and be away from Raven's Peak for a night. Nora gave him an odd look when he requested a single room with two beds.

"Miles—"

"I'm not leaving you alone, it's too dangerous," he said in a tone that brooked no argument.

She met his gaze with a wary look but didn't protest, making him wish he'd worn his shades in case she glimpsed the hungry man beneath his stony face. Did she feel the intense chemistry that he did between them?

A few minutes later, they walked down to the riverfront, found a pub and slipped inside. Miles wolfed down a shrimp po' boy while Nora nibbled on a seafood salad. The water lapped at the shore as they walked back to the motel, the sights and sounds of Savannah surrounding them. The carefree tourists hadn't a clue that a serial killer was stalking the South. Or that ghosts roamed their quaint Southern town, and that the neighboring islands housed a questionable research park with secrets that some would kill for.

A street musician wailed out blues music while jazz floated from a nearby restaurant. Wind whistled along the bay and lovers rushed hand in hand toward their cars, not lingering to stroll as they would in the spring or summer. He imagined the town alive with tourists in April, with spring flowers, blooming azaleas and romance, a life he didn't think existed. Then they passed a graveyard and reality slid back into focus.

Nora quickened her pace, her eyes wide as they passed the statues and tombstones. Ghosts whispered from the graves, reminding him that death could claim her any minute.

Suddenly from nowhere, a gunshot rang out, and pinged off the wrought-iron gate encasing the cemetery.

Nora screamed, and he grabbed her and pushed her down to her knees. He drew his weapon and searched the darkness, the shadows of the live oaks nearby, the Spanish moss draping the ground like spiderwebs. Another shot pinged near their heads, and Nora scrunched closer to him while they darted behind a park bench. A couple of teenagers suddenly ran the opposite way, and Miles motioned for an elderly man who was approaching to run.

The shooter fired again, and Miles cursed. Someone was trying to kill them.

NORA WAS SHAKING ALL OVER as Miles shoved her behind the bench. Who was shooting at them? Someone from Nighthawk Island? The person who'd killed her sister? Dr. Hollinsby?

Miles scanned the shadows and she cut her eyes over the graveyard, hunting, searching for the shooter. A shadow moved stealthily across the graveyard, ducking behind monuments, a ghostlike creature that made her wonder if he was real or a figment of her imagination.

But the shots had been real.

Miles fired at the shadow, and another shot zoomed toward them. He fired back, protecting her with his body. Footsteps pounded on the pavement. He released her, then stood and dashed toward the corner, but a black sedan sped the other way. She ran to him on wobbling legs.

"Did you see him?"

Miles muttered an obscenity. "No, and the car didn't have a tag." He unpocketed his phone and punched in some numbers. She burrowed deeper into his coat while he relayed the incident to Detective Black.

The urge to hide, to run and never come back to this town, needled her. But they had to wait on the police to come and search for the bullets.

When the police arrived Detective Black assured them the police would do what they could, but Miles shook his head. "He was a hired professional," he said. "I don't think we'll find him."

"I'll have Agent Devlin check into ex-military trained snipers. Maybe he works for someone on Nighthawk Island." Detective Black narrowed his eyes. "You must be on to something or they wouldn't try to get rid of you."

"Shooting at us won't stop me from uncovering the truth," Miles barked. "I'm going to find out what they did to Nora and Caitlin if it kills me."

A shudder rippled up Nora's spine. Miles almost sounded as if he cared about her. But he was just doing his job. He loved her sister.

And she wouldn't be able to live with herself if he died because of her.

She had to remember what had happened the night she met Caitlin at the bar….

Finally the police finished, and she and Miles hurried back to their motel room.

She was so cold inside, had been ever since she'd escaped Nighthawk Island. The thought of burying her sister, the realization that she had almost died tonight and that Miles had protected her, had her nerves raging. She hurried into the shower to warm herself, then stood beneath the hot spray of water and let the tears fall. Tears of fear and grief. Tears for Caitlin. Tears for herself, and for the baby Caitlin had lost. Tears for Miles and the pain he'd suffered.

Tears because she wanted him and couldn't have him.

Guilt and self-loathing filled her as she dried off and pulled on a robe. But when she stepped into the bedroom and saw Miles staring at her, his jaw set, his powerful body so rigid with self-control and emotions, more tears surfaced.

"Nora?"

"I'm sorry…it's just been a long day."

"I know."

His rigid body screamed of barely controlled rage, and intense anger simmered beneath the surface. Then their gazes locked and something hot flashed between them. A need so strong that Miles suddenly strode toward her. She fell into his arms, trembling, aching with wanting him. He soothed her with soft whispers, stroked her hair, held her to him. She couldn't resist, she turned her lips into his palm and kissed his hand. Their gazes locked again, the tension rippling between them. Then he lowered his head and pressed his mouth to hers. A low groan erupted from deep within her, as if she were dying and only he could save her.

The kiss was tender, passionate, full of questions and tentative longing. Or maybe his reaction was born of compassion.

She didn't care.

She wanted him to kiss her so badly she thought she might drop to her knees and beg him to continue if he stopped. His hand dove into her hair, tangled in the already unruly tresses, and she angled her head back to allow him better access while his lips played along her mouth, then down her neck. His mouth came back to hers, and his tongue probed between her lips, plunging, exploring, tasting, teasing. She moaned and met his tongue with her own, dancing along his lips with the tip as he pulled her closer. Her breasts pressed against his chest, the sensitive tips tightening as his hand slid down her back, over her waist, then upward to cup her in his palm. He made a throaty moan of his own, and she smiled against him, gliding her fingers along his muscled back and arms. He was all power and strength, all male hardness. All heat and passion.

A low ache mounted in her belly. She wanted him closer. To have their bodies naked, slick with want and hunger, to set their minds free to ride the waves of raw passion.

He inched her backward until her knees brushed the back of the bed. She didn't argue. Didn't fight the yearning deep inside her. Instead, she let him lay her back onto the bed, let him lick and kiss the blinding ache away as he dipped his head lower, pushed her sweater up, released her bra clasp, and latched onto one nipple with his mouth. The sound of his suckling splintered her last thread of resistance, and she arched toward him, begging him for more.

Praying he would take her all the way to heaven.

SOME PART OF MILES'S rational brain warned him to stop, that touching Nora was wrong. That Nora had only needed comforting. That her tears had not been an invitation to take her to bed.

But the fact that someone had tried to kill them shattered his control. He wanted to prove to her that she was still alive, that she could still feel pleasure.

He teased the tip of her nipple with his tongue, his body hardening with desire as she arched toward him. He had to oblige. Tasting and loving her right breast with his mouth was heavenly, so he slid his other hand to the opposite globe and tormented her there, finally licking his way over her turgid nipple. She clawed her hands into his hair as if she couldn't get close enough, and he suckled her harder, finally leaving her breasts to trail kisses down her belly. She moaned and fire blazed through him. With deft movements, he removed her clothes. The sight of her dark curls and soft femininity nearly undid him. He licked the insides of her thighs, delving his fingers into her curls, then spread her legs and teased her warm, wet sex until she cried out for him to stop.

But he refused.

He pressed tongue lashes along the insides of her thighs, inching his way to her sweetness, and flicked his tongue over her wet center, teasing and torturing her. At the same time, he slid a finger inside her heat, spread her legs farther apart, filling her, sliding his fingers in and out as he ached to do with his sex. Over and over, faster, harder, building the tension. Her throaty moans coached him to plunge deeper, deeper, until finally he delved his tongue inside her. She exploded in his mouth, spiking his senses into a frenzy with her cries of pleasure.

Euphoric, she thrashed against the covers, her hands clenching the bedcovering as she rode the waves of her orgasm. He licked the glistening moisture from her inner thighs, something moving inside his chest when he looked up and she opened her arms to him.

He tore off his shirt, then moved above her, pressing his sex into her heat.

But something else flared in her eyes—uncertainty.

He held himself in check for a moment, studying her face, the same face that belonged to the woman he'd married, the one who'd betrayed him. The same face he had fallen in love with. The one he wanted beside him now.

But this was her look-alike. What was he doing?

Nora had been traumatized, was burying her sister tomorrow. The lines blurred, the two women's faces interchanging.

"Miles?"

Her voice quivered with recognition. She knew he was thinking about her sister. The woman he'd married. Knew that the lines were blurred, his feelings, hers, a mess of tangled emotions and lies.

Despair and pain flickered in her expression, then she pulled away from him.

He cursed himself, but he let her go.

NORA DROPPED HER FACE into her hands and rocked herself back and forth on the edge of the tub, shame washing over her. What in the world was she doing?

Falling into bed with Caitlin's husband, letting him touch her intimately, practically begging him for more. She had never behaved so wantonly with a man before.

Because she'd never wanted a man as much as she wanted Miles.

Was it because he had married Caitlin?

No.

She stood and faced the mirror. The face that stared back reflected a mixture of Nora and Caitlin—two identical women with memories of both.

But they had been different as children. Different as young adults. Had grown apart.

For a moment, the world tilted sideways, and she saw an image of herself with Miles. Walking hand in hand together in the rain. Window-shopping. Kissing beneath an ancient oak tree. Bodies entwined as lovers.

Then the image disappeared, and she once again studied the mirror, more confused than before. Had she just had a memory? And if so, when had she walked hand in hand with Miles? When had they window-shopped?

She rubbed her head, willing her mind to focus and sort out the truth, but pain shot through her temple, and she felt as if she were looking at a stranger. Her cheeks were flushed from excitement, her lips swollen from Miles's kisses, her body still tingling with the aftermath of the pleasure he'd given her.

She couldn't deny her feelings any longer. She was falling in love with him.

Self-recriminations resurrected the little voice in her head. *You're the bad twin, always jealous of your perfect sister. Always wanting what she had.*

And now she wanted Caitlin's husband. And she hadn't even buried Caitlin yet.

A sob lodged in her throat, and she dropped her head forward, ill to her stomach. How could she be so selfish when her sister's life was over?

A knock sounded at the door. "Nora?"

She closed her eyes, willing the floor to open up and swallow her. What was she going to do? How could she face Miles after the way she'd behaved?

"Nora, please come out. We need to talk."

She inhaled sharply, splashed water on her face, then

grabbed a towel and wrapped it around her. She couldn't let him see her naked and exposed again.

And whatever she did, she couldn't reveal her true feelings toward him.

GUILT EXPLODED in Miles's chest as Nora finally emerged from the bathroom, the sight of her nearly naked in that towel resurrecting the painful surge of longing that had throbbed in his sex only minutes before.

The throb that still ached for her. But a relationship with her was impossible. There were too many questions. Too many memories of Caitlin. Too many secrets and lies.

Nora refused to look at him, but reached for her clothes. He could see her getting ready to bolt again. She was ashamed of what they'd done, of offering herself to him.

No matter what she thought of him, he couldn't allow her to blame herself.

"Nora, I'm sorry."

She froze, her hands gripping her sweater. He dragged his gaze away from the delicate skin of her back above the towel, then she turned to look at him, and he nearly groaned again when he spotted a water droplet clinging to the soft swell of her breasts.

The breasts he had suckled earlier until she'd writhed in his arms.

His body hardened.

Jesus, he needed to put some distance between them.

"I don't want to talk about it."

He strode toward her, grabbed her arms and made her look at him. "Well, we're damn well going to."

"Miles, stop, just let me go…."

"No." For God's sake, he'd screwed up, but he couldn't

let her berate herself for needing consoling. "Listen, I shouldn't have touched you, taken advantage of you."

"No, I'm sorry," she said in a ragged whisper. "I...I've never behaved like that before." A flush stained her cheeks, giving her such an innocent look that his legs nearly buckled. Heaven help him, she was just like the woman he'd married, the Caitlin he'd first met. Sweet. Caring. Sensitive. Honest.

But this was *Nora*...

"Don't apologize for feeling," he said gruffly. "For needing a friend."

Her gaze met his. Her eyes were so clear, brimming with emotions, embarrassment, heat, fear...and something else. He wanted to believe it might be tenderness, or even...love, but he couldn't allow himself the luxury.

No one had ever loved Miles Monahue before. No one except his parents, and they'd died when he was ten.

He dropped his fingers from her arms, hating himself for still wanting her, for needing her so badly. "Look, it's been a rough day for both of us. Let's drive back now. I'm too wired to sleep, but maybe you can rest in the car." He cleared his throat, knowing he sounded cold. Like a bastard.

Well, hell, he was a bastard. He couldn't stay in this room with her and not have her.

"What we did—it's only normal," he continued, his voice adopting a hard edge. "Sex relieves stress."

She flinched at his blunt words, then bit down on her lip, worrying it with her teeth. "It can't happen again," she said in a strained voice. "Not ever."

"You're right." He sighed heavily. "I...it won't happen again."

The silent truce they formed reverberated with tension as they gathered their things and headed to the car.

DR. HUBERT HOLLINSBY studied the early morning newspaper headlines, the coffee he'd just sipped burning an
acidic path down his esophagus as he skimmed the
article.

Late yesterday afternoon after a conference with
medical examiner Dr. Arthur Mullins, sources
revealed the identity of the murdered woman found
at Devil's Ravine. When her body was first discovered, she was thought to be Caitlin Collier Monahue,
the wife of Raven's Peak's Sheriff Miles Monahue,
but when a look-alike showed up claiming she was
Caitlin Collier, police believed the dead woman to
be her twin sister, Nora. Now, police have confirmed
that the woman was indeed Caitlin Collier Monahue.
Police are still questioning suspects, and investigating to determine the twin's reasons for impersonat-
ing her sister.
   Even more interesting, police have confirmed
that the MO of the murder is identical to that of the
serial killer stalking the South, yet police are not
certain if Mrs. Monahue's death was the result of the
elusive Carver or a copycat.

Hollinsby crumbled the paper in his fists, pushed away
from his secretary's kitchen table and grabbed his jacket.
He knew the police had been looking for him at his office,
and they'd been to his home. And White had left him
several messages—the very reason he'd chosen to spend
the last two nights in his secretary's bed. The police didn't
yet know about his affair with Jayne, but given enough
time, they would. Just like they'd eventually find out about

his work, his past and the experiments with Caitlin and Nora Collier.

Then he would be in big trouble.

He had to get the hell out of town. No, out of the country. Sure, he'd be leaving valuable unfinished projects behind, but another government abroad would hire him. Once he established an alias, that is. Some of them would probably pay him more than the U.S. did. And they wouldn't be so picky and concerned with red tape that he couldn't work on a few cutting-edge side projects that the U.S. hadn't yet sanctioned.

But he had to handle this problem with the Collier woman first.

Twisting his mouth in thought, he grabbed his keys, a plan formulating in his brain. He had to get Nora Collier alone, determine how much she remembered. Keep her from exposing the truth about him.

No matter what he had to do to her, he'd protect himself and his work. A chuckle rumbled from his chest. Every scientific genius had to make sacrifices.

In the bigger scheme of things, Nora Collier was just a nanomolecule in the macrocosm in which he existed....

Chapter Thirteen

Dawn broke as Nora and Miles arrived back in Raven's Peak. They passed an early-morning church service on the lawn and she considered asking Miles to stop. But Miles's window was cracked, and the preacher, a man named Reverend Perry, had shouted about marriage and fidelity, and she'd clamped her mouth closed.

But not before seeing the pain on Miles's face.

Inside the cabin, Nora stood at the edge of the bedroom door, listening as Miles gripped the phone to his ear. He was talking to the federal agent. Another woman's body had been found.

Tina Hollinsby—she was dead. Nora felt it in her bones.

Miles mumbled that he'd meet the federal agent at the crime scene just as Nora entered the den. She was determined to go with Miles. He could drop her in town afterward, and she'd find a place to stay.

She had to extract herself as much as possible from his life. Last night, after that close call at the island, then in the cemetery, they had almost crossed the line and made love. She had finally dozed in the car, but Miles had driven most of the night. This morning he looked exhausted and worried.

She wanted him more than life itself.

Miles hung up the phone, scrubbed a hand over his face, his forehead furrowed.

"They found another victim?" she asked softly.

He jerked around at the sound of her voice. "Yes, Tina Hollinsby. I have to go. Stay here until I return."

"Let me go with you."

His dark eyes met hers. "No. You don't want to see this."

She flinched. "Then drop me in town. I'll find a room at a motel. You know I can't continue to live here with you."

"We'll talk about it after I return." He gestured toward the fireplace. "Go to bed, get some rest."

She watched him stalk out the door, then paced to the window. How could she be safe when her sister's killer was on the loose?

Chilled, she stripped her clothes, turned on the hot water, then stepped into the shower. While she lathered her hair and rinsed it, she mentally formulated a plan. She'd have to find a place to stay, but she needed a job. Maybe Miles could help her obtain some ID and loan her enough cash for a deposit on an apartment. Although she didn't want to owe him anything.

An icy thread knotted her stomach as she considered the other tasks in front of her. She had to talk to the funeral home and make arrangements for Caitlin's burial today.

A sudden noise jarred her from her thoughts. Had Miles forgotten something?

She turned off the water, grabbed a towel and wrapped it around herself, then tiptoed to the bathroom door to listen. Nothing.

Breathing a sigh of relief, she donned a robe and

headed toward the bedroom, but just as she knelt to gather her clothes, the floor squeaked. She pivoted to check out the sound, but someone grabbed her from behind.

Nora screamed and lashed out, but the man threw a pillowcase over her head so she couldn't see, then tried to drag her backward. She kicked and swung her fists, grappling for something to use as a weapon. Her fingers connected with the lamp and she swung it up, catching her attacker in the side. He grunted, his grip relenting slightly, and she kicked backward and connected with his shin.

Gasping for air, she threw off the pillowcase and ran to the door. Not bothering to look back, she darted outside. She hadn't seen her attacker, but she didn't intend to wait around and let him kill her. Pumping her legs, she tore into the woods, desperately wishing for shoes as her bare feet hit the icy ground. But there wasn't time. He was right behind her. She dove through a thicket of pines, racing over bramble and stumps and dead leaves. She had no idea where she was going, but she had to get away.

She didn't want to end up like Caitlin or Tina Hollinsby.

SOMETHING NAGGED at the back of Miles's subconscious as he drove down the mountain. Another woman was dead. And the MO matched the work of The Carver.

He had to find the sick SOB, then let Nora go. She had gotten under his skin. Had made him feel things for her he didn't want to feel.

Made him want her.

So, he'd run. But she was in danger.

What if the killer knew where he lived? He could be waiting until Miles left Nora alone....

And like a damn fool he had.

Just like Caitlin, he was letting emotions—no, lust—for Nora distract him from his job.

He slammed on the brakes, swerved onto a ramp for runaway eighteen-wheelers and turned around, then sped back up the mountain toward his cabin. The trees flew past in a brown maze, his heart pumping so fast he heard the blood roar in his ears. What if he was too late? What if the killer already had her?

He'd lost Caitlin to the madman; could he lose her sister?

The tires squealed as he skidded on black ice. He down-shifted into low as he maneuvered the sharp curve. Ahead, dark clouds loomed in the early morning sky, threatening another storm, casting a gray gloominess over the horizon.

A minute later, a flash in the woods near his cabin caught his attention. A deer?

No, a person. He yanked the wheel to the right, and glanced sideways, slowing as he scanned the woods. The figure darted in between the trees.

Then he saw a swish of long dark hair. A woman's pale form. She was in her robe, running as fast as she could through the thick weeds.

Nora.

Swerving into the end of his drive, he threw the car into Park, checked his weapon and darted into the woods. His eyes scanned the bushes, the trees, the embankment to detect who she was running from.

At first, he saw nothing. No, there was a shadow in the distance. A man. He was chasing behind her a good hundred feet.

Miles dashed into the thicket, weaving in and out between the oaks and pines, heading toward the impasse to cut her off. Leaves crunched and twigs snapped beneath his feet. Birds squawked in the early morning sky. A deer cocked its head, then bolted away seeking safety.

The man was gaining on her. Closing in. Miles raised his gun, aimed and fired.

The man suddenly disappeared behind a tree. Nora screamed and ducked behind a cluster of thick pines. Miles aimed again, his next shot pinging off the tree where the man had hidden. Then the man ran again, ducking and taking cover behind the trees, heading toward the highway. Miles started to chase after him.

But he couldn't leave Nora.

He turned and scanned the woods, called her name. "Nora, it's me! Miles!"

He inched forward, searching the brush. "Nora!" A squirrel skittered up a tree. His boots pounded the icy vegetation. "Nora, it's all right. He's gone."

His breath caught in his throat as he circled to the back of the weedy patches surrounding the pines. He spotted her crouched down on the ground, hugging her knees to her chest. When she looked up, her eyes met his, her irises black with fear. She was trembling all over, her breath puffing out in a white cloud, her pale skin pink from the cold and exertion.

His heart slammed against his ribs. She looked so damn lost and frightened, like a vulnerable little girl. And her skin was already turning blue.

He tugged off his jacket, gently wrapped it around her shoulders. She stood slowly, hugging the coat around her. "He was in the house when I got out of the sh-shower."

He tilted her chin up with his thumb. "Did you see his face?"

She shook her head, her trembling growing more intense. "No, he attacked me from behind."

He glanced down then, saw her bare feet against the stark white snow. Knew she was freezing. He had to get her out of the elements.

So he swung her up in his arms. She protested, but he ignored her and stalked down the path toward his car, cutting across the woods in a shortcut. His chest heaving for air, he hugged her close, trying to warm her with his body against the wind, and wishing he could kill the bastard who'd attacked her.

TIME PASSED in a surreal state as Miles carried Nora into his cabin. He immediately built a fire, grabbed blankets, and wrapped them around her, then brewed some hot tea and made her sip it.

"Are you okay?" he asked.

"Yes," she managed to whisper. Her body was warming, the chill of fear and the elements slowly evaporating as another kind of fear possessed her. Fear that she wanted Miles when she should be thinking about finding this killer. And burying her sister.

Realizing the dangerous train of thought, she stared into the crackling flames.

He lifted his hand to touch her cheek. "Did he hurt you?"

The concern in his gruff voice tore at her already thready restraint on her emotions. "No, I'm okay, really. I just wish I'd seen his face so I could identify him."

"We'll get him," Miles said quietly. His hand dropped to her neck where a bruise had already started to turn purple. "I promise you, Nora, he won't touch you again."

Nora nodded. She itched to reach out and touch his

cheek, to ask him to hold her, but she had to resist. When he looked at her, he saw her sister. His wife. The woman he'd loved. Not her.

Caitlin's shadow.

A HALF HOUR LATER as they drove toward Devil's Ravine to meet Agent Brown, Miles's pulse was still racing. When he'd seen those bruises, the urge to fold Nora in his arms, to kiss her until the fear evaporated from her eyes, had almost overwhelmed him. Just the sight of Nora's terrified face twisted at hormones already raging out of control. His need for her was growing stronger.

But she wasn't his wife. He had no rights to her. No reason to trust that the chemistry between them was any more real than the volatile reaction he'd experienced with her twin.

His hands gripped the steering wheel of the Pathfinder, his Ray-Bans in place, the tires churning the black ice as he wound around the mountain. He scanned the highway and woods for signs her attacker had returned or was following them, and felt the anger rippling through him, heating his bloodstream, firing his temper.

Nora remained silent, her arms folded, her gaze riveted to the mountains passing by in a blur. When he parked at Devil's Ravine, he left her in the Pathfinder and crossed to the gorge. Agent Brown, the profiler Agent Adams, Dr. Mullins and several crime-scene investigators were already there, taking pictures, DNA samples and searching the area for clues.

"You found her?" Miles asked.

Agent Brown gave a clipped nod. "She was a little farther downstream, but the MO's the same. I've issued an APB for her husband. We have agents stationed at the airports, train stations, bus routes and rental-car agencies."

"Does he have a passport?"

Agent Brown nodded. "We already sent an agent to his house. Some of his clothing and personal belongings are missing."

"Did they find the trophies The Carver took?"

"No, no sign of any wedding rings."

Miles grimaced. "He's on the run."

"Which makes me think he's guilty."

Miles chewed the inside of his cheek. "Someone attacked Nora Collier at my place."

Agent Brown's eyebrow shot up. "When?"

Miles explained about leaving her, then returning. "He was chasing her through the woods."

"Did you get a look at him?"

"I wish to hell I had," Miles muttered. "And before you ask, neither did she. He put a pillowcase over her face and tried to drag her outside, but she escaped."

"Send the pillowcase to forensics, we'll see if we can get anything off it."

"When I get back, I'll dust for fingerprints, but I doubt we'll find any."

Miles walked over to where Tina's body lay, his gut clenching at the sight of the bloody *A* carved into her chest. White lilies dotted the water just as they had with Caitlin.

"Did he take anything?" Miles asked.

"Her wedding band is missing just like the others."

Miles turned to the female agent. He'd heard she was a profiler. "What's your take on The Carver?"

Agent Adams tapped on her notepad. "He's intelligent, educated, probably early thirties. He probably suffered sexual abuse by one of his parents, perhaps the mother. His conscience told him it was wrong to have relations with his mother, yet his body responded, so now he has mixed feelings about sex and women.

"He had a strong religious upbringing, and believes he's saving these women somehow. The lilies represent purity. He takes the wedding rings because the women have broken their vows and no longer deserve to wear them."

"But how is he choosing his victims?" Miles asked. "Is it a random act?"

"At first sight, the original five victims appeared to be random," Agent Brown said. "The only connection between the women was that they committed adultery."

Miles blew air through his teeth. "Both Caitlin and Tina Hollinsby were seen at the Steel Toe shortly before they went missing."

Brown cleared his throat. "I'm going back there myself and question everyone."

"Was Hollinsby in Savannah or Atlanta at the time of the other murders?" Miles asked.

"I have an agent investigating that now," Brown said. "Hollinsby traveled on a speaking circuit last year, so it's possible he was in both cities."

"Where were you last night?" Brown asked.

Miles glared at him, but he had an alibi, so he filled him in on his trip to Nighthawk Island.

"Did anyone at CIRP corroborate Nora Collier's story?" Brown asked.

"No, but they've been known to cover up research experiments and unethical conduct before. Why should I believe that Hollinsby didn't this time? After all, someone tried to kill us after we left the island. And someone attacked Nora Collier earlier at my house."

Miles's mind raced. The religious angle of the serial killer disturbed him. If this guy was so religious, how could he justify murder? "You said the killer has a religious background. Have you considered that he might be a member of the clergy?"

Brown and Agent Adams exchanged odd looks. "We explored that angle in both cities. In fact, we questioned a priest in Savannah, and a televangelist in Atlanta, but the leads didn't pan out."

"Although the televangelist pointed out the scripture that refers to the white lilies," Agent Adams said.

Miles chewed over the possibilities. There was one Baptist preacher in town, Reverend Sutherland, but he was in his early fifties. He definitely didn't fit the profile of The Carver. That young guy, Reverend Perry, had preached about marriage and infidelity, but he was the son of a local, and Miles didn't recall him being out of town the last few months. Still, he should talk to him.

And a Catholic priest had recently moved to town— Father Flemming.

If The Carver was a religious fanatic and thought he was doing God's work, maybe he felt compelled to repent afterward. Then he might seek out a priest for confession....

Father Flemming. He'd question him and see if he'd received any interesting or disturbing confessions lately.

Confessions from a killer trying to save himself after he committed murder.

Chapter Fourteen

A half hour later, Miles parked at the funeral home. After they finished their business here, she had to convince him to let her stay at a hotel. Being near him was becoming increasingly difficult. She wanted him to touch her and hold her and look at her with affection, with love, but that avenue was a dead-end road.

He studied her for a long moment, his expression hooded. "Are you ready to go in?"

Nora nodded, although anxiety intensified the knot in her stomach as she climbed from his car and walked up the sidewalk to the funeral home. The last thing she wanted to do was to be here, choosing a casket and handling the details of her sister's burial.

Inside, soft classical music wafted through the speakers. The white walls were clean, adorned with colorful pictures of gardens in greens and mauve that matched the comfortable sofas and chairs scattered throughout the parlor to the left. She spotted the funeral director's office to the right and knocked on the door.

A short balding man who could have been anywhere between thirty and fifty appeared in a three-piece suit, a slender handsome younger man with strawberry-red hair and green eyes beside him.

"I'm Nora Collier. Caitlin Collier's sister."

Both men appeared momentarily startled. Hadn't they heard that Caitlin had a twin?

The younger man recovered first. "Yes, Miss Collier, Sheriff Monahue. So sorry for your loss."

"Come in and sit down," the bald man said. "I'm Lonny Mortimer, the funeral director."

"Reverend Perry." The young man smiled and shook her hand, his grip loose. "Can I get you some water, coffee, a soda maybe?"

Miles declined, and Nora shook her head. She wasn't certain her stomach could even handle water.

"Do you have a cemetery plot?" Mr. Mortimer asked, looking back and forth between them.

Nora knotted her fingers around the edge of her sweater. "Yes. Next to my parents in Ellijay." She glanced at Miles. "That is, unless you want to bury my sister here."

His eyes darkened with pain, reminding her of the baby her sister had carried. "She should rest with your family," he said in a gruff voice.

She gave the funeral director the details of her parents' resting place, then braced herself as he led them to choose a casket. Dear God, could she really do this? Could she bury her sister, her best friend, the one she'd shared the secret language with when she was a little girl?

MILES GRITTED HIS TEETH as Nora chose a steel-gray casket with ivory satin lining, his thoughts scattered. Plush carpet, soft music and the hint of flowers added an ambience to the occasion as if to disguise the fact that death vibrated through the quiet crème-colored rooms.

And that his wife lay in the crypt downstairs because of a sadistic serial killer.

While Nora excused herself to visit the ladies' room, the funeral director pulled him aside. "I'm going to help Miss Collier with the arrangements. Put her in touch with the local florist, encourage her to think about what she wants engraved on the tombstone. That is, unless you want to handle things." He cleared his throat. "After all, you're the husband."

Miles grimaced. His marriage had been so short, he didn't feel he had the right. "No, I want her to make the decisions."

Miles shoved his hands in his pockets. "Will you keep her here for a while? I have business in town, and I want to make sure she's safe."

"Certainly. This is a difficult process for family members." Mortimer's eyebrows formed a unibrow as he frowned. "Losing a wife is hard and I'm sure losing an identical twin is devastating."

"Yes, she's having a rough time." He didn't mention the fact that she'd been drugged, hospitalized and that someone was trying to kill her.

Nora exited from the restroom and headed toward them, her body hunched within itself. He explained that he'd be back to get her, then went to talk to Reverend Perry before he acted foolishly, put his arms around her to console her.

It was so damn hard not to look at her and see his wife. The woman he'd fallen in love with.

The woman who had betrayed him.

Yet, dammit, he wanted her anyway.

The real Caitlin or her look-alike…he wasn't sure it mattered. The lines had intersected now, become entangled.

He found the young preacher in the chapel, comforting another couple who'd lost their grandfather in an accident. A few minutes later, he pulled Perry aside and asked if he'd known Caitlin or Tina Hollinsby.

"No, I'm afraid neither of them attended my services." He spoke in a hushed, almost reverent voice. "I wish I could help them somehow. I'll do everything I can to comfort their families in this crisis."

Miles managed to broach the subject of the night before without raising suspicion. Reverend Perry claimed he was counseling the family who'd lost their grandfather, and when he left the man, the daughter confirmed his story.

Wind whipped at Miles's hair and stung his cheeks as he stalked to his car. The sleepy little town that had once seemed safe now reeked of suspicion and murder. The people who were neighbors and friends, who'd never met a stranger, looked around warily, rushing inside their houses to lock doors, distrust shadowing their faces as if the town had now been tainted. And it had. A killer was hiding in these mountains, perhaps in an old abandoned cabin, perhaps in one of the houses right on Main Street in clear sight. A killer who was cunning and smart, one who didn't mind taking lives.

One who had to be stopped before he murdered another woman.

Before he hurt Nora.

His hands tightened on the steering wheel as he veered

into the parking lot of the small catholic church. What the hell was he thinking? He couldn't have a relationship with his deceased wife's look-alike....

THE ANGUISH Nora experienced after viewing her sister's body congealed inside her, turning her shaky emotions into a fireball of rage. After setting a memorial service for the following afternoon, ordering flowers and choosing a short epitaph for Caitlin's tombstone, she was drained and exhausted. She'd seen herself in that casket, and it increased her awareness that death might be whispering her name.

"I have to get some fresh air." She headed toward the door, but Mr. Mortimer stepped in front of her, blocking her exit.

"Please, wait, Miss Collier. The sheriff requested that you remain here until he returned."

Panic clawed at her, claustrophobia mounting. She was being held in a room, imprisoned, the scent of sickly flowers…no, medicines or some kind of cleaning solution suffocating her. She couldn't stay here any longer.

"Please, I have to go." She pushed him aside, then practically ran from the funeral home. Outside, the bitter cold assaulted her. Wind tossed dead leaves across the street like tumbleweeds in a deserted ghost town, and tears scalded her face and stung her eyes. She didn't know where to go, but she kept walking. Across the square, beside the graveyard where ghostly images danced in the shadows, then past a hair salon called Curl Up and Dye, until she spotted the Steel Toe, the honky-tonk where she had met Caitlin.

Memories of their childhood entertainment shows

flooded her as she entered the smoky bar. She and Caitlin had played dress-up in their mother's old prom dresses and high heels, created a makeshift stage and sung country tunes at the top of her lungs. Then when they were eight, they'd fashioned a stage outside and invited the neighborhood children to watch them perform, charging a quarter for a seat, and upgrading their selection of tunes to include more contemporary rock hits.

Caitlin had laughed and clapped along, although she'd been much more shy in front of the crowd. Instead, she'd sold tickets and helped the younger kids find seats, kids she later worked with in day camps in the summer.

The noisy din of laughter and drinking shattered her reverie as she strode through the sea of men. Country music crooned from the jukebox, a few early afternoon patrons playing pool in the back, gathering for drinks and smoking cigarettes. A small voice inside her head taunted a warning that stepping inside this place was dangerous, but she refused to let fear deter her. There wasn't a soul in the world left who cared about her. And she had to right the wrong that had been done to Caitlin.

She slid onto a bar stool, well aware several men turned to glance her way, although she certainly didn't intentionally send out vibes of interest. But maybe she should. If she played up the seductress role, maybe she could lure the killer into her hands.

Then she'd call Miles and let him arrest the bastard.

The same bartender she and Miles had spoken with the last time they'd visited, Jimmy Joe, smiled and raised an eyebrow, then handed her a scotch. Hmm. She sipped it, and frowned, then ordered a glass of white wine.

He gave her an odd look. "I thought scotch was your drink."

A distant memory flirted with her subconscious. Nora liked beer, scotch; Caitlin preferred wine. Or had it been the other way around?

What had they done in that hospital to scramble her memories?

"Where's the sheriff?" Jimmy Joe asked with a coy smile.

She shrugged, pretending nonchalance. "Working, I guess."

The bartender leaned forward with an interested look. "I thought maybe you and he were, you know, together."

She offered a lilting laugh. "No. He was my sister's husband, that's all." And no matter how hard she tried, she couldn't be her twin's replacement.

"Are you staying in town?" he asked.

She shrugged. "Maybe. I really need a job."

"You want to wait tables or sing, you're hired."

She smiled and sipped her wine, letting her eyes rake over him. "That would be great. When do I start?"

"How about tomorrow night?"

"That should work." She angled her stool to study the other patrons while he tended two husky motorcycle guys in black leather pants and vests. The cowboy, Buck, who'd supposedly slept with her sister, sat back, looking lazy and half drunk at a corner table. So far, Miles hadn't been able to pin anything on the man, but she still didn't trust him.

Suddenly the bartender appeared again and slid a folded piece of paper in front of her.

She glanced at him in question. "What's that?"

"Someone left it for you."

She scanned the crowd, eyeing each of the men nearby. "Who?"

"Didn't see him. The waitress brought it over, said she found it on one of her tables."

Nora's stomach fluttered although she assured herself it was silly to be nervous. It was probably some cheesy pick-up attempt by one of the half-looped customers.

But when she opened the note, her breath caught in her lungs.

Dear Nora,
Your sister was a very bad girl, a whore. One of the secret society trying to spread sin in town.

But a marriage vow is a sacred, holy union. "Till death do us part."

She broke those vows and had to be punished.

Do you need saving like your sister?

MILES HADN'T BEEN in a church in years. Not that he was proud of the fact that he'd drifted away from what little religious upbringing he'd had, but after his parents had been murdered he'd been shipped to his grandmother's, then that group home, and he'd never found his way back. He wasn't certain he even felt comfortable walking inside a holy house now.

But he was desperate for answers. He had a town to save, a killer to catch and his job to earn back.

Soft candlelight flickered from the front of the church, and an older woman and her husband lit a candle, then knelt at the altar for prayer. He spotted a young teenager slip into the confessional box, then draw the curtain closed.

Confession was supposed to be good for the soul.

Should he admit to Father Flemming that he was lusting after his dead wife's sister?

He remained in the corner, hidden by the shadows of the polished woods and statues of Mary, until the young boy emerged. His head ducked low, a ball cap shading his eyes, he hurried toward the rear of the church as if he didn't want to be seen in the sainted place.

Miles approached quietly, not wanting to disturb the praying couple, then ducked inside the confessional box. He drew the curtain, wishing he could draw one on his emotions as well. Instead, he tapped on the window. "Father, I need to talk to you."

"Yes, my son. How long has it been since your last confession?"

"I'm not here for confession, Father Flemming. I need to discuss the Carver case with you."

A long pause. "I'm not sure what I can do for you."

Miles explained the profiler's theory about the serial killer. "I'm aware of your vows," Miles said. "But Father, if someone has confessed to you about one of these murders, you have to tell me."

"I'm sorry, Sheriff, I really am, but I can't help you. If you have sins you'd like to confess—"

"My wife is dead," Miles said in a gruff voice. "Along with another woman in town. Both at the hands of a sadistic killer who may be stalking his next victim now. Tell me, has someone spoken to you about the murders?"

Tension stretched between them, but the Father didn't respond. Miles stormed from the confessional box, then rapped on the priest's door. Father Flemming appeared, looking agitated, rubbing at his collar as if it were too tight around his neck.

Guilt? His conscience maybe?

"Father, please —"

"I'm sorry, Sheriff. The confessional is sacred. If I break my vows, then I'm breaking my word to God, and I'm of no help to the needy in my parish."

"And what if another woman dies?" Miles crossed his arms, his expression stony. "How will you live with her blood on your hands?"

Father Flemming flinched, then crossed himself. "It is in God's hands. We must trust in him above all others."

Miles barely stifled a curse. Maybe that was the problem—he didn't trust anyone.

Not himself. Not the woman he'd married or her sister. Not even the priest.

His cell phone jangled as he stepped outside into the blustery wind. "Sheriff Monahue."

A long silence, then a breath. "Sheriff, this is Donna Perkins from the research hospital on Nighthawk Island."

He froze, his gaze tracking the street as if he thought she might be nearby. "I'm listening."

"I heard you were asking questions about the Collier twins."

"Yes?"

"I'd like to talk with you in private. I…might know something."

"What?"

"One of the twins was at the hospital on Nighthawk Island."

Miles wheezed a breath. "As one of Dr. Hollinsby's patients?"

"Yes. But there's more. I have to see you."

"Tell me—why was she there?"

Noises sounded in the background. Voices.

"Please, it's too dangerous." Her voice wavered. "I'm leaving town. I'll meet you tomorrow and explain everything."

"Stop by the funeral," he suggested. It was as safe a place as any.

"All right, I'll see you then."

"Miss Perkins?"

She hesitated. "Yes?"

"Be careful."

She agreed, then hung up, and he hurried to find Nora to tell her about the call. But when he entered the funeral home, the director informed him that she had left.

He gripped the man by the collar. "Where did she go?"

"I don't know." The man wiped his forehead with a handkerchief. "She was upset and darted across the street. I tried, but I couldn't stop her."

Miles stared out the window, then up and down the town square. What if the killer was here in town, waiting, watching? What if he kidnapped Nora and killed her as he had Caitlin?

NORA'S HANDS TREMBLED as she clutched the note. She scanned the men at the bar for a familiar face, then pivoted and noted the blur of male faces situated at the tables.

Had one of them sent the message? Was Caitlin's killer here now, watching her?

A squirrely man with bushy eyebrows gazed at her, bleary-eyed over a mug of beer. Another, two stools down, nursed a whiskey, his lanky leg jiggling as he zeroed in on her mouth. To the right, a cowboy wearing a double R on his belt buckle threw up a finger in greeting. Buck leered at her, then winked.

Anger churned in her stomach. The killer was a coward. He was taunting her. Sending her a note, while hiding behind the faces of the local patrons. He could be any one of these men.

Had Caitlin known him? Had she trusted him, accompanied the man willingly, then ended up his victim?

"Hey, sugar. Can I buy you another drink?"

Nora jerked her head sideways and was greeted by a cocky smile from another stranger. This man had longish brown hair, a small scar over his right eyebrow, sandy brown eyes that reminded her of the desert. Suddenly every man in the bar looked like a killer.

She tapped her nails on her leg. "Sure."

He motioned to the bartender, who gave an eyebrow lift, but sent another glass of Chardonnay her way. She gripped the fine stem of the glass to keep her hands from trembling, then forced herself to ask. "What's your name?"

"Abel." He licked the head off his draft beer. "What's yours?"

She almost said Caitlin. "Nora. You new in town?"

He grinned. "Naw. Just passing through."

"What do you do?"

"I'm a trucker. First time to deliver in Raven's Peak, but I'll be back." He scooted closer, until she inhaled the musky scent of his cologne. "Especially with pretty girls like you being friendly."

Nora had thought she could do this but she was wrong. She loved her sister, but after meeting Miles, she couldn't stand the thought of another man's touch.

She pushed away from the bar and stood, but the man grabbed her arm. Then she glanced up and saw Miles walking toward her.

THE SIGHT OF THE MAN'S HANDS on Nora sent white-hot rage through Miles. It made no sense that he wanted her so badly when he couldn't have her.

Yet he didn't want another man to have her, either.

His reaction wasn't fair but he couldn't help himself. She looked so much like the woman he'd fallen in love with. Felt just like her. And she needed him.

The other man stood and faced him as if he understood the silent challenge.

"She's with me," Miles said flatly.

Nora's eyes darted to him, then the other man.

He angled his head toward her. "Is that right, sugar?"

She licked her lips, then nodded, and the man threw up his hands as if to indicate he didn't want a fight. It was a good thing because Miles was spoiling for one.

He gripped Nora by the arm and moved her toward the door. "What in the hell are you doing?"

"I had to get away from the funeral home," she said, pulling at his hand to release her.

"Flirting with a stranger is not safe and you know it." He paused in the alcove by the pay phone and restroom. "Have you forgotten that a maniac named The Carver is out there? You remember what he did to your sister?"

Her face blanched, and regret slammed into him with the force of a sledgehammer. "I'm sorry," he said, lowering his voice. "But I don't want to bury you, too."

Her breathing sounded choppy in the ensuing silence. "He took my sister from me," she whispered. "I had to do something." Then she raised her head, and looked into his eyes. He tried to mask his emotions, but he felt as if they were etched on his face for all the world to see.

His own confused emotions were mirrored in her eyes.

Then she withdrew a piece of paper from her purse. His blood ran cold as he read the message.

It was from The Carver.

He had been in the bar watching Nora.

And he was coming for her next.

Chapter Fifteen

Miles intended to send the note to forensics and have it tested for prints. Maybe they could analyze the handwriting, the ink, the paper. In fact, something about the way the man had printed the letter *A* struck him as familiar. The Carver had written the letter with the same slant as this man had.

He'd seen someone else slant their *A*'s that way—but where?

He met the bouncer at the door. "I don't want any man to walk out of this bar until I have his handwriting sample."

Of course, The Carver might have already snuck out the door before he'd arrived, but he had to follow every lead. The man just might be in the room watching their reactions, laughing, hiding behind the anonymity of the local establishment.

He phoned his deputy, who arrived within minutes to take the samples. Nora watched cautiously from a corner table, and he kept an eye on her as well, scanning the room constantly for anyone looking at her suspiciously. Of course, half the men in the place were tuned in to her every move. She was a beautiful woman. Irresistible. A siren wailing out a silent song of seduction without even realizing it.

But he had to ignore the call.

An hour later, his deputy had collected samples from everyone, including the bartender and bouncer, and he placed them in a bag to send to Agent Brown. He phoned him and they agreed to meet at his office.

"Are you ready?" he asked Nora.

She finished the glass of wine she'd been sipping and nodded, then stood and pulled on her coat. They walked in silence through the crowded bar, the stares of the patrons burning Miles's back. If one of the men inside the Steel Toe was The Carver, he had to stop him before he hurt Nora.

He slid his hand protectively to the small of her back as they stepped outside. Granted, he couldn't have her, but he'd die before he let her meet her sister's fate.

NIGHTMARES PLAGUED NORA'S SLEEP. Nightmares of her hospital stay. Of the drugs and the shock treatments. Nightmares of being watched, hunted down by a crazed killer. Nightmares of feeling that knife plunge into her heart and tear her life from her.

Just as it had her beloved sister.

She could almost feel her sister's pain. Her last breath whooshing from her chest...

The next morning she moved on autopilot as she and Miles stopped at the department store to buy Nora a dress for the funeral, and to purchase one for Caitlin. The day before, the director of the funeral home had suggested dressing Caitlin in a dowdy black dress that someone had donated, but Nora couldn't allow her sister to be buried in something so ill-fitting and inappropriate. She'd even mouthed the sentiment that Caitlin wouldn't be caught dead wearing a dress like that, then realized her crass comment and felt a fresh wave of tears surging behind her eyes.

Miles simply nodded, paid for the items, then drove her to the chapel. She was surprised to see a handful of floral arrangements beside her sister's coffin, and noted that Miles had ordered a heartshaped spray of roses, another reminder that he had loved her sister. The Steel Toe employees had sent a cross of carnations, and Buck had sprung for a mix of fresh flowers. But the arrangement closest to the casket made her gasp.

A basket of white lilies.

She gripped Miles's arm. "My God, do you think the killer sent those?"

Miles's muttered curse answered her question. Agent Brown confiscated the basket, then contacted the florist to determine the sender.

Seconds later, Agent Brown had a response. "Not much luck. They were ordered from a one-eight-hundred number. We're trying to track down the credit card owner."

"It's probably stolen," Miles said. "Our killer isn't stupid enough to leave a paper trail."

"You're probably right," Brown said.

Reverend Perry shook Miles's and Nora's hands. "I'm sorry for your loss. Try to remember that she's in a better place."

Nora nodded quietly. Miles muttered something beneath his breath, while a small gathering of spectators who must have read about Caitlin's death, people who'd heard her sing, bustled in and gathered in the chapel, catching Nora's attention. She'd been so afraid the service would be empty.

"Let me know if you see anyone you recognize," Agent Brown told Nora.

Nora searched the group hoping for some familiarity but a sea of strangers' faces swam before her.

"The killer sometimes shows up at the funeral," Miles explained in a low voice. "It's a part of his sickness, he can't stay away."

She gulped and nodded, her gaze tracking the room. Buck sat in the back, along with the bartender and a couple of the waitresses. Oddly, Dr. Mullins, the medical examiner, slid into a pew in the back row.

"I'm surprised he's here," she said as Miles led her to the front row.

Miles frowned and slanted his gaze toward him. "Sometimes M.E.'s get caught up in the investigation. They like putting the pieces of the puzzle together. Mullins is one of those."

He liked to play cop.

"I'm going to talk to that young preacher, Reverend Perry, after the service," Brown said.

"He is new in town," Miles said. "And he's giving a special series of sermons on marriage and fidelity."

Brown's eyebrows shot up suspiciously.

Nora shivered at the thought of the preacher hurting her sister, and they quieted as a young woman began playing the strains of "Amazing Grace." Reverend Perry rose and began to preach about sin and redemption, his gaze aimed at Nora as if he were speaking directly to her.

Had he killed Caitlin?

Miles's mouth tightened, and he folded his hands,

dropping them between his knees. Nora felt so alone, she ached to reach out and cling to him, but she had no right. He had married Caitlin, and had to mourn the loss of his wife.

And she had to grieve for her sister, all alone.

MILES STRUGGLED with a barrage of emotions as he and Nora stood around the grave site, but his hand moved over his pocket and the charm bracelet felt heavy against his palm. He still couldn't believe the woman who'd been so excited over it when they'd bought it together, who had cried when he'd whispered that he loved her, was gone.

"Hopefully, I'll hear something this afternoon on that note and handwriting analysis." Brown cleared his throat. "And Monahue, we did find another connection to the victims."

Miles jerked his gaze up, grateful the agent had slacked off on pointing the finger at *him*. "What?"

"Each of the women visited this Web site called 'Swinging.' It started as a secret-society-of-swinging-singles site but has morphed into something bigger. Groups meet online and then form swingers groups in the cities, small towns."

Miles frowned. His wife had visited that site? "You mean married couples?"

"Yes." Brown cocked his head sideways. "Our killer takes the wedding rings of his victims. Maybe he's trying to put an end to the swingers group."

"Jesus." Miles glanced at Nora's ashen face and ached to go to her. "I suppose tracing our killer from the people who visited the site is near impossible."

"I have a team of experts working that angle, review-

ing any posts that might have opposed the swingers' lifestyle, but researching the site list will take time. Besides,
our killer is smart. He probably pretended to be one of
them so he wouldn't raise suspicion."

"But you are looking at the victim's computers?"

"Absolutely." He folded his hands in front of him. "Did
Caitlin have a computer?"

Miles shook his head. "No, and I checked out mine
when she first went missing. Checked her e-mails, online
status, hoping for a lead, but it was a dead end." Resent-
ment surged through him. The feds and Brown had also
checked his computer and Brown knew it.

The song ended and so did their conversation.

Nora tugged a scarf around her neck while the cemetery
workers spread the flowers across her sister's grave. He
moved up to stand beside her, searching the graveyard for
the nurse who'd called, but he didn't spot her anywhere.
Had she made it to Raven's Peak? Or had something
sinister happened to her?

Exhaustion and pain lined Nora's face. He wanted to
fold her in his arms. But with the combustible chemistry
between them, he was afraid if he did, he wouldn't be able
to release her. And when they arrested this psycho, The
Carver, they both had to move on.

Nora knelt and dropped a yellow rose petal on her
sister's grave. "I love you, Caitlin," she whispered, dab-
bing at the tears on her face. "You're still with me, and you
always will be."

Miles clutched his hands by his sides. Even if he and
Nora wanted to be together, her sister would always stand
between them. The lines were too blurred, their faces too
identical.

And when he'd nearly made love to Nora, when he'd tasted her lips and her body, she had tasted just like his wife.

NORA COULD NOT BELIEVE the killer had sent white lilies to her sister's funeral. Rage blazed through her, pushing her grief to the back of her mind as her fury took center stage. Damn this man for killing Caitlin, and now for toying with her like this.

Miles drove back to his office in Raven's Peak and introduced her to his deputy, a tall, brooding man named Tim Long with black hair, ice-blue eyes and a cleft in his chin. "I'm going to meet Agent Brown at the forensics lab," Miles said. "Stay here with Deputy Long, and I'll be back."

"Why can't I go with you?"

He shook his head. "You look exhausted. And I have work to do. Once I meet with Brown, I intend to search the town and see if I can find out if that nurse ever showed up." He paused. "Now stay put. You remember what happened when you left the funeral home."

A chill tickled her spine at the reminder.

She read his unspoken words. He thought the woman might be dead and wanted to spare her.

He gave his deputy a sharp look. "Keep her safe."

Deputy Long nodded, and Miles turned and left.

Nora felt as if she were under a microscope as the deputy studied her.

"I'm sorry about your sister," he said in a gruff voice.

She nodded and sank into the wooden chair but a plan formulated in her mind. The killer wanted to taunt her, had been at the Steel Toe the day before. Would he go back again?

Anger surged through her as she battled her helplessness. She had to do something. She just couldn't sit here and twiddle her thumbs.

"It's been a rough day. I could use a drink," she said.

"We have bottled water in the fridge."

"I mean a real drink," she said in a soft voice. "I'm going to walk over to the Steel Toe."

He stepped in front of her, his body braced in an intimidating stance. "You heard the sheriff. You're not going anywhere alone."

She shrugged, brushed her hand across his chest, then walked past him. "Then come with me."

His stumped expression indicated he hadn't expected her audacity, but she was through being the victim here, the confused needy woman. She wanted to avenge her twin's death.

He caught up with her and walked beside her, his expression grim as they crossed the street, passed store fronts, then entered the bar.

"Do you really think this is a good idea, Miss Collier?"

It was the best one she'd had in days. She intended to regain the power she'd lost. Any action was certainly better than trailing after her sister's husband like a lovesick puppy.

Nora liked scotch. She ordered a glass, then tossed it back with a scowl, and ordered another. The bartender and deputy were both watching her, but she didn't care. She wanted to look vulnerable right now, wanted to bait the killer enough to make him approach her.

"Ready for some entertainment?" she asked the bartender.

"Sure, sugar. The guys would love a song."

Jimmy Joe slid around the counter, grabbed the mike

and introduced her. "Ladies and gentlemen, we have a treat tonight. Nora Collier is going to sing for us. Give it up for her."

Clapping, shouts and catcalls erupted, and she braced herself, a moment of stage fright assaulting her. Her nerves pinged inside her as she stepped up to the microphone. Nora never had stage fright, only Caitlin. The thought came in a rush to her head, but she quickly dismissed it and wet her lips. It was time for some action.

A minute later, she was lost in the moment as she crooned the words to "Strawberry Wine." She poured her heart into the song, then finished to the sound of more clapping and shouts for an encore. She smiled at the men, searching their faces, wondering if one of them might be a killer.

Silently, she begged him to approach her.

"NO FINGERPRINTS on the note," Agent Brown told Miles. "But we're still working on the handwriting analysis. And I'm going to run a background check on Reverend Perry. See if he was in Atlanta or Savannah at the time of the previous Carver cases."

Miles's phone trilled, and he answered it, his brain trying to assimilate the fact that the small town preacher was a suspect.

"Sheriff Monahue, it's Donna."

He breathed a sigh of relief. "You didn't show today."

"I thought someone was following me on the way into town. But…I lost them."

"Can you meet me now?"

"Yes. I'm in that little coffee shop across the square in town. Clara's."

"I'll be right there."

Miles offered Brown a clipped explanation, then strode out the door. Five minutes later, he entered Clara's Cafe, and scanned the diner for a stranger's face. Clara poured coffee into a mug, then carried the coffee along with a piece of her famous apple pie to a booth in the corner. He followed her movements and spotted a short, robust woman huddled in the vinyl seat, looking anxiously toward the door. She nearly dropped her coffee mug when he approached.

"Donna?"

She nodded and glanced nervously at the door again, scooting back into the seat.

"Are you all right?"

"Yes, I guess I'm just nervous. When I left Savannah, I thought someone was behind me. Then again, when I drove around the mountain, a car was following me."

He slid into the booth. "What did you want to tell me?"

She fluttered a hand over her chest. "I heard you and Miss Collier came to Nighthawk Island to investigate her hospital stay."

"Yes, and we were told she was not a patient."

She glanced down at her cup, then poured a packet of sugar in it and stirred vigorously. "That's not true."

He arched an eyebrow. "She was there then?"

"Yes. I helped take care of her myself."

"I see. Why was she hospitalized?"

"Her file indicated that she'd suffered a twin identity crisis."

"Dr. Hubert Hollinsby was her doctor?"

She nodded. "He took a special interest in Miss Collier."

"Donna?" Miles reached out a hand to stop her nervous

fingers from thumping on the table. "Did he hold her there against her will?"

Her eyes grew wide, frightened. "That's hard to say. Many of our psych patients try to escape."

"Was she ill when she was admitted?"

"I don't know that, either." She fiddled with her purse. "But he paid me not to tell anyone her name. That's when I figured out that something wasn't right. She didn't belong there."

"No, I don't believe she did."

Donna sniffed, wrestled into her purse, then withdrew a folded paper. "I found this, just to prove she was there. See." She pointed to the form and his eyes narrowed as he skimmed it.

"This says that Nora Collier admitted herself."

The woman nodded. "That's what Dr. Hollinsby told me. You see, I think he was having an affair with either her or her sister. He kept her heavily sedated. And he conducted some experiments on her, ones he wouldn't discuss."

That revelation didn't surprise him. But the fact that Nora had admitted herself for treatment did.

She had lied to him when she'd first approached him for help. And if she'd lied about that, what else had she lied about? Maybe she really was mentally ill and needed help. Maybe she had suffered an identity crisis....

He had to confront her, find out why she'd concocted that bizarre story. Find out if she had seen Caitlin the night she'd disappeared.

His phone trilled, and he apologized to Donna for the interruption. "It's my deputy, I have to take it."

She nodded, and picked at the pie while he connected the call.

"Monahue, it's Tim. Listen, after you left, Miss Collier insisted on leaving, too."

"And you let her?"

"I'm with her now."

"Where?"

"At the Steel Toe."

Catcalls erupted in the background along with loud jeers. Miles cursed, an image of Nora on stage assaulting him, taking him back to the night he'd met Caitlin. An image of the other men lusting after her followed, making his gut pinch. Then one of The Carver raising a knife to take her life slammed into him, and he stood, his heart pounding.

"I don't know what she's doing," Tim continued, "but she had a couple of drinks and now she's on stage—"

He muttered a string of obscenities. "I know exactly what she's up to," he snarled. "She's trying to lure The Carver into coming after her."

Chapter Sixteen

The door swung open and Miles strode inside the bar, his senses alert. He removed his shades and sent Nora a stony look. Nora halted momentarily, then turned a soul-shattering smile toward the audience.

Had anything that had happened between them been real, or had she been playing him all along?

She crooned the words, "I Will Always Love You," in the softest, sexiest voice he'd ever heard, the very song Caitlin had sung the night they'd met. She was toying with him, trying to seduce him, along with the other men in the audience.

A surge of unadulterated rage fired his bloodstream at the sight of her strutting around the stage. When his deputy had called him to relay what she was doing, he'd nearly lost his breath. She was hurting, desperate, dangerous right now.

He had to stop her from her crazy plan.

He strode forward to drag her off stage, but his deputy threw out a hand. "I've been watching the crowd. She's all right."

But what if the killer had gotten her? He'd failed her

sister and she'd ended up dead. He couldn't fail Nora, too, or she might suffer the same fate.

Her ruby-red lips purred out the words in a sultry voice that catapulted him back to the night he'd met her look-alike. The night he'd thought she was singing to him. But he couldn't be fooled. He had to harden his heart, or it would be broken all over again.

She finished the song with a flutter of eyelashes, then kissed her fingers and waved as if she were tossing the men a kiss. They went wild.

He moved like lightning and manacled her arm in his hand, then dragged her back to the alcove by the bathroom. "Do you want to end up in the grave beside your sister?"

Grief flashed into her eyes, and he regretted his words, but he had to do something to scare her. Or maybe she did want to die? Maybe she was so distraught that she didn't care about her life.

But he did, dammit.

She blew a strand of hair from her eyes. "I'm not going to just sit around and let this maniac pull the strings. If he wants me, then let him come after me."

"Nora…please." He lowered his voice to a pleading tone. "It's not worth taking the chance—"

"He's murdered seven women so far, Miles, and the police haven't found him. *Seven.*" Tears glistened in her eyes but she blinked them away. "I want him caught."

He turned her hand over in his palm, then traced circles with his thumb. "So do I. But not at your expense."

She pulled away, her heart in her eyes, and he felt sucker punched again, as if he'd been looking into Caitlin's eyes, touching her arm.

He had to tell Nora that she'd committed herself to the hospital. Maybe hearing the truth would trigger her memories of meeting Caitlin that night.

But what if she hadn't remembered because she and her sister had fought? What if she was dead set on catching this killer because she felt guilty over her twin's murder?

Nora liked to play twin switches.

His gut tightened. What if Nora had been the one online at that swinger's group? What if the killer had thought that he had kidnapped Nora instead of Caitlin—had he killed the wrong twin?

NORA WOBBLED TOWARD the restroom, nearly tripping over her heels in her escape from Miles. For a brief second when she'd seen him enter the bar she'd wanted him to know she'd been singing to him.

But he hadn't noticed or responded. And she had felt like a fool.

She washed and rinsed her hands then glanced at her reflection in the mirror. Her face looked like Caitlin, innocent, sweet, loving. Why did she feel like the face fit, but that the act she'd just performed in the bar was totally an act? That she didn't belong on stage in front of lurid men, that she didn't like the attention?

She dropped her head forward in her hands, wishing she could straighten out her tangled memories. But she'd lost her mind in that mental ward and she didn't know if she'd ever get it back.

Shaking off her self-pity, she reapplied her lipstick, touched up her makeup and fluffed her hair.

On with the plan.

But just as she stepped from the bathroom, a firm hand

shoved her from behind. At first, she thought it was Miles, but a voice growled low in her ear. "Yell, and you die."

She froze, a chill skating over her, but he shoved her forward with a fisted hand. She started to scream, but he grabbed her arm, twisted it behind her, then pressed his other hand to her mouth. "I said, be quiet."

Behind her, music from the jukebox wailed out a country song. Laughter and voices blended into the night. His hand tightened around her arm until she thought he'd wrench it from the socket, and she winced in pain, stumbling as he kicked open the back door. The back parking lot was empty, and her heels clicked on the pavement. She dug them in, determined to fight for her life, to get a look at his face.

He pushed her toward a dark sedan, and sent gravel spewing. Panicked, she gripped his arm, then kicked upward at his groin, but he dodged the blow. He reached for the car door to shove her inside, but suddenly a shout erupted into the darkness.

"Stop it right there! Police!"

The man hurled her forward. She threw out her hands to catch herself as she fell, but her palms hit the concrete, her knees next with a sickening thud. Footsteps pounded the pavement, then Miles jumped her attacker and she heard the sharp crunch of bones.

Hollinsby.

His face was seared into her consciousness. Miles sent the man flying with his fists, then tackled him to the ground. She wobbled toward them, then noticed that Miles's hands were bleeding where he'd punched Hollinsby's face. Blood spurted from Hollinsby's nose, and his eye was turning black.

She pressed her hand to his back. "Miles?"

His loud exhale filled the tense silence, then he reached inside his coat pocket. "You're under arrest, Dr. Hollingsby." He jerked the man to his feet, then his dark eyes found hers. "Are you all right?"

She nodded, shakily. "Yes, I am now."

They exchanged a moment of understanding, then he recited Hollinsby his Miranda rights as he pushed the man toward his SUV.

Nora followed, her breathing erupting in choppy little waves. She didn't know if Hollinsby was The Carver. But at least he could explain why she had been locked in that god-awful mental ward.

Maybe during one of the sessions she had confided what had happened the night she'd met her sister at the bar, the last night her twin had been seen alive.

MILES POUNDED THE TABLE in front of Hollinsby in the interrogation room. They'd been at it for over an hour, and Hollinsby hadn't broken. "We're on to your sick game, Hollinsby. Tell us what you did to the Collier twins."

Hollinsby's thin lips pinched together.

Agent Brown leaned into Hollinsby's face. "Did your wife find out about your affairs? Is that why you killed her?"

"And why the others?" Miles persisted. "The women in Savannah, Atlanta. We know you visited that swingers Web site. Is that how you chose your victims?"

Hollinsby was sweating, but he curled his long skinny fingers around the edge of the table. He'd clammed up the minute they'd gotten to the station and hadn't said a word.

"I want a lawyer."

Miles cursed silently while Brown shot Hollinsby a murderous look. The room smelled of sweat, frustration and lies. Yet Hollinsby had the gall to stall.

"Look, Hollinsby," Miles barked, "I caught you red-handed trying to kidnap Nora Collier—"

"I just wanted to talk to her," he protested.

"Then why drag her outside with a gun?"

Hollinsby cut his eyes sideways, then down to his hands. "Because I knew you were looking for me. But I'm not that psycho killer The Carver, and you're not going to pin those crimes on me."

Miles gripped him by the collar. "Is it true that Nora admitted herself to the hospital?"

Hollinsby gave Miles a sour look, but tugged at his sleeve nervously. "I refuse to say another word until I have a lawyer present."

Brown thumbed a gesture for Miles to meet him outside, and Miles bolted through the door ready to tear someone's head off.

"I can't believe that guy," Miles snarled. "Leave me alone with him for just five minutes."

Agent Brown shook his head. "No way. I'm not going to let you blow this investigation because of your temper. If this guy has killed seven women, we have to play it by the book."

"But—"

"No buts, Sheriff," Brown said. "You're too personally involved here. Take Nora Collier, go some place and keep her safe for the night. I'll call you if I persuade him to talk."

"But I want the truth about what happened to my wife."

For the first time since he'd met him, Brown relented and gave him a sympathetic look. "We'll find it. Just trust me and let me do my job."

Miles stared at him long and hard, his temper fired. Yet Nora was waiting in the office, alone. She'd been through hell today and probably needed a shoulder to cry on, or at least some rest. And Brown was right—he couldn't botch the case and let the man go free on a technicality. Caitlin deserved to have her murderer caught and imprisoned—or dead from a lethal injection.

Miles clenched his hands.

He'd be happy to administer it himself and watch the man die.

SNOW FLURRIES SWIRLED in the frigid air as Nora and Miles drove back to his cabin. The scenery passed in a blur as the day's events traipsed through her mind. The funeral. Saying goodbye to her sister. The bar and Hollinsby's hand clamped around her wrist. The realization that he might take her back to that awful hospital.

Or that he might have killed her.

"He didn't explain anything?" she asked, grasping for some sliver of a reason why he'd locked her in that mental ward.

A muscle ticked in Miles's jaw. "No. He denied being The Carver. That's all he said, then he lawyered up." He patted her hand, and she curled her fingers around his and squeezed.

"Thank you for saving my life, Miles."

He parked in front of his cabin, killed the engine, then turned to her, his eyes hooded. She sensed he planned to say something, but he simply stared at her, then opened the door and climbed out. A weariness unlike anything she'd ever known tugged at her limbs as she pushed from the car, and they hurried through the blustery winds up to his cabin. Inside, he lit a fire, and she gravitated toward it, trying to warm her hands.

"Nora—"

She turned to him, her pulse quickening at the distress in his somber eyes.

"I know you think my actions were stupid," she said in a low voice. "But I feel so helpless. I want to catch my sister's killer. I…want her back."

Tears choked her then, and she dropped her face into her hands, sobs wracking her body. He pulled her into his arms, and pressed her head against his chest.

"Shh, I know…"

Nora sank against him, exhausted and drained, scared out of her mind. He stroked her back, rubbing low circles until some of the tension dissipated. Still, she clung to his arms, inhaled the woodsy scent of his masculine body, the fresh smell of laundry detergent, the coffee on his breath as he leaned his head against hers. He felt so wonderful, so strong, she couldn't drag herself away.

He held her while she cried, until all her tears were spent. Then when she thought he would pull away, when she ordered herself to, he tipped her chin up with his thumb and brushed the moisture from her cheeks with his fingers. "I feel so alone," she whispered. Like she was going to shatter any minute and evaporate like ashes in the wind. Her parents were dead. Caitlin, her twin, the other half of her soul, was gone, too.

He lifted her chin and his mouth found hers. "You aren't alone, Nora. We've got each other."

If only that were true. But his heart had belonged to Caitlin.

The cold fear that had overwhelmed her the minute

she'd felt Hollinsby's hands dissipated in Miles's warm embrace. She'd never felt anything so right, as if she belonged with him, as if he'd been ripped from her before and she'd found her way back to him.

The raw passion in his endlessly dark gaze turned her into a quivering mass of desire as if he'd physically touched her just with one look of his eyes. She wanted him. Needed him.

Caitlin was gone. And she was here now.

If he closed his eyes and saw his former wife, what did it matter? They had both loved her, they would mourn her together, and comfort each other through the lonely night.

Telling herself she didn't care, but knowing it was a lie, she lifted one fingernail and traced it across his jaw. She wanted to be the woman in his arms tonight, the sexy vamp, the woman to assuage his pain.

He groaned when her hand touched his face, closed his eyes as if straining for control or a reason they shouldn't be together. She placed a delicate kiss along his cheek, then another and another, teasing him with gentle tongue flicks, whispering her desire as she threaded her hands into his hair.

One second they were standing in front of the fire in the den, the next they were sprawled on the braided rug. Moonlight spilled into the cabin through the small window, white snowflakes dotting the window panes and painting crystalline patterns on the glass. The fire crackled and popped, the flames flickering across his handsome face as he lowered his head and kissed her over and over. Heat simmered and blazed through her body just as it did through the room, driving them together, bringing them closer to one another in the dark hours of the morning and night.

Passion and raw, potent hunger laced his every movement as he tore her clothes from her and threw them across the room. His clothes went next, until their naked skin collided, the sensations rippling through her sultry and erotic. He traced the contours of her mouth with his finger, then dipped his tongue lower to tease the soft globe of her ear, and lower to her neck. His hands trailed down, caressing, stroking every sensitive inch of her naked body, exploring, teasing, tweaking her nipples to hard peaks that stood rigid, begging for his mouth.

"Please, Miles."

He answered with a flick of his tongue across her breasts, then he closed his mouth over her nipple and sucked hard, biting, kneading her with his hands, growling as she clawed at his arms to be closer. He took her on the floor, spreading her legs wide, then rising above her to watch her face as he rolled on a condom, then sank his length into her. She cried out as he filled her, then whimpered as he lowered his head and kissed her again. He caught her moan with his mouth as he thrust himself deeply within her. She circled her legs around him, binding him into the crevice of her body, moaning as he thrust inside her, pulled out, then thrust deeper and harder, building a blinding rhythm that sent titillating sensations splintering through her. A minute later, he roared his release, clutching her hips upward so they were bound together as they both climbed to heaven.

MILES WAS ON THE VERGE of whispering Caitlin's name when he caught himself. This was Nora.

Only she tasted, felt, made love like his wife.

Because he wanted her to be or because she was? Hell, maybe he was the one who needed therapy.

He rolled to his side and cradled her in his arms. He wanted the moment to last forever, wanted to hold her until dawn came and went, until they could forget about the past and a killer and that her sister lay between them.

Their breathing rattled in the quiet, the fire embers hissing as they fell asleep in each other's arms.

Sometime later, in the heat of the night, he awakened. The fire had burned out. The room had turned cold. But Nora still lay in his arms. She twisted and looked up at him, and emotions pummeled his chest. He wanted her again.

She wanted him, too.

He swept her up in his arms and carried her to bed, the two of them sliding beneath the covers to cuddle, to hug and lick and tease each other all over again.

She suddenly crawled on top of him, then cupped his face in her hands. "Miles...I—"

"Shh." He pressed his fingers to her lips. He didn't want words. Didn't want to have to explain or for either of them to apologize.

She smiled although her eyes looked moist with tears, then he made her forget their reservations as he captured her mouth with his own. She skimmed hungry fingers up the insides of his thighs, and his body jerked in response, his sex surging toward her. She cupped his length in her hand and stroked him, then traced a path down his belly with her tongue. He moaned and she bent her head, licked the moisture at the tip of his sex, and he threw her onto her back, flipped her over and crawled above her, splaying his hands along her back. He massaged her shoulders, her spine, her lower back, lifted her enough to cup her breasts, then teased her buttocks with his sex. She stretched her hands above her and he entwined his fingers with hers as he intended to do with their bodies.

Their coupling was wild, erotic, frenzied, fantastic. He wanted the night to last forever.

NORA NEVER WANTED the night to end, for Miles to stay inside her all night long, filling her, making her complete, loving her until they were both mindless with pleasure. He thrust inside her again, whispering erotic words in her ear, then licked her neck and made a sucking noise until she cried out for him to go harder and faster. He pounded inside her, lifted her to her hands and knees and drove them both mad as he plunged into her again. Her breath was ragged, her cries of passion primal as waves of ecstasy crashed inside her.

She whimpered his name, begged him to continue, pulled at his hips to make him sink deeper. Their passion was cataclysmic. She couldn't help herself, she shouted his name, then that she loved him.

He hesitated momentarily, but they were too far gone for him to stop. Instead he intensified the movements, his erection plunging deeper, his hands teasing her senseless, his hunger raw and primitive, as he groaned and met her in oblivion.

Seconds later, when she thought he would leave her, he cradled her in his arms and held her.

"Miles—"

"Shh." He traced a finger over her cheek and snuggled her into his chest, then placed his head on top of hers and kissed her hair. "We'll figure it out tomorrow."

She sighed and stroked her finger across his hair-dusted chest. She'd take tonight if that was all he had to offer.

MILES CLOSED HIS EYES, his chest tight with emotions. He had no idea what had happened. He had brought Nora home from the police station, yet he was almost certain that he'd just made love to his wife, Caitlin.

He had to question Hollinsby again, had to figure out what he'd done to the twins.

Find out for sure which one they'd buried, and which one he was holding in his arms now.

Chapter Seventeen

Sunlight streamed through the window, blinding Nora as she opened her eyes. It had been an earth-shattering twenty-four hours. Her sister's funeral. Hollinsby's attack. Making love to Miles.

She wanted to love him again. Being intimate with him had felt so right, as if she'd been in his arms before, as if that was where she belonged.

She rolled over to snuggle into him, but the bed was empty. She pressed a hand to his pillow where it was still warm, already missing him, then glanced up and saw him standing by the window. His shoulders were squared, his body rigid as he stared outside.

"Miles?"

He turned toward her then, and another wave of hunger seized her. He was dressed in a pair of low-slung jeans, his bare chest glistening with water droplets as if he'd just showered. His dark hair was still damp, making her itch to run her hands through it. And the scent of his soap and male body made her body clench with desire.

But he had those Ray-Bans back on as if he needed to hide his face. His expression. The need in his eyes.

His jaw went rigid, then he tightened his fingers around his coffee mug. He already had regrets.

"Miles—"

"Shower and get dressed," he said in a gruff voice. "We're going to talk to Hollinsby this morning. He's finally going to tell us the truth about everything."

She licked her dry lips, aching for him to come to her, to say something personal, to assure her that they could work things out. Being with him had felt so natural, she couldn't imagine not having him in her life.

But he strode past her into the kitchen, leaving her alone with her questions. For her, making love had brought them closer together, it had bound them as one.

For him, making love had driven them further apart.

MILES'S MIND WAS ON OVERLOAD, spinning with different scenarios as he and Caitlin faced Hollinsby in the interrogation room.

She trembled when they walked in, then raised her chin in defiance as if she refused to let him frighten her again. He gripped his hands into fists, ready to attack the man if he so much as attempted to touch her.

Hollinsby's lawyer, Whittaker, sat beside him. He was a tall, heavyset man with gray hair and jowls that flapped when he introduced himself. Agent Brown joined them and steepled his hands on the table.

"You have a deal for my client?" Mr. Whittaker asked with narrowed eyes.

"It depends on what he tells us," Agent Brown said.

"He's not your Carver," Whittaker said, leaning forward. "But he does have information about Miss Collier that might help you find the killer."

Brown made a noise through his teeth. "I'm listening."

"We want answers," Miles said. "And I want Miss Collier to hear, too. Hollinsby agreed." Miles produced the hospital admittance form he'd received from the nurse. "Explain this."

Hollinsby's face turned ashen, and he ran his fingers through his thinning hair. He looked ten years older than he had the day before.

"Did Nora Collier admit herself to the hospital for psychiatric care?"

Nora gasped beside him, then shot Miles a shocked look. He probably should have told her about the form, but uncertain what to believe, he'd kept the information to himself.

Hollinsby worked his mouth from side to side. "No."

"What do you mean?" Miles asked. "This is her signature, right?"

He gave his lawyer a wary look, but the lawyer gestured for him to talk.

"Nora signed that paper, yes. But she wasn't admitting herself. She was admitting her twin sister, Caitlin."

Nora gasped again, and Miles gritted his teeth. He'd put together that scenario in his head on the drive to the station.

"Tell us what happened from the beginning," Miles said. "How do you know Nora and Caitlin Collier?"

Hollinsby gave his lawyer another questioning look.

"Go ahead," Whittaker said calmly. "You talk, they'll deal."

Brown nodded, and Hollinsby folded his fingers on the table. "I met Nora through this swingers Web site. After we talked online for a while, we decided to meet in person."

"Then you had an affair?" Miles asked.

Hollinsby's lips thinned. "Yes. I…she was irresistible. We saw each other for a while, met at the Steel Toe. That's where a lot of the swingers hook up."

Miles's mind raced. Brown was checking into that site, maybe they were onto something. The killer chose his victims from the group.

"Go on," Brown said.

"Nora…after I got to know her, I discovered she had a twin. She also had some issues…problems."

"With her identity?" Miles asked.

"Yes. With jealousy." He offered her look-alike an apologetic look. "Some twins are close, while others are conflicted. They have a love/hate relationship with their twin, suffer feelings of inferiority, sibling rivalry, jealousy. Nora fit into that category. She had trouble establishing her individual identity and felt she lived in her sister's shadow." He paused, his breathing labored.

"She came to me one night, hysterical. She said her sister had just married, and she was ranting about how unfair it was, that Caitlin got everything." He shuffled nervously, twisting his mouth again. "Then she admitted she was pregnant."

"Nora was pregnant?" Brown asked. "I'm confused. I thought our deceased twin, Caitlin, was pregnant."

Miles threw his hand up in warning. He was piecing together the events in his mind, he just wanted to hear Hollinsby admit it. "Let him finish."

"She knew I had conducted research on twins, and that I'd worked with identity crisis cases. In fact, I tried to help her deal with her issues with her sister. I suggested long-term therapy, but she resisted. Then she wanted to end our relationship."

"But you didn't want to do that."

He shook his head, skewing his mouth sideways. "No, but she blackmailed me, threatened to tell my wife about our affair unless I helped her."

"Helped her how?" Miles asked.

"She was considering an abortion. I begged her not to."

"Because you thought the baby was yours?"

"I…wasn't sure." He cut his eyes toward Nora again. "Then she came to me, upset because her sister had called her and invited her to her wedding. Nora was jealous. She refused to attend. But three days after the wedding, she phoned her sister and asked her to meet her at the Steel Toe."

"I remember us meeting there," Nora said. Her face paled, and she suddenly stood and crossed the room. "Oh, dear heavens, I remember now, we argued about the abortion. I didn't want her to have it…." She turned to Hollinsby, the truth dawning. "I offered to take the baby and raise it if she'd carry it to term. I told her that I'd talk to Miles—"

"She's Caitlin, isn't she?" Miles asked in a gruff voice.

Hollinsby coughed into his hand, then nodded. "Nora drugged you, Caitlin. Then she called me." He dropped his head forward and continued in a strained voice, "I took you to the facility at Nighthawk Island."

Miles's heart hammered in his chest. "And you drugged her and restrained her there so she wouldn't discover her sister's devious actions?"

Hollinsby nodded again. "I switched files, medical charts, to confuse the twins' identities in case someone came looking for her."

"What else did you do to her?" Miles asked.

A long-suffering sigh escaped Hollinsby. "I've always been interested in the psyche of twins, so I decided to try an experiment. I spent enough time with Nora to understand her thought processes, and she'd confided enough of her past, situations between the two of you, her feelings, so…" He glanced up at Caitlin, a sick smile twisting his lips. "I hypnotized you and gave you her memories. At one point, I convinced you that you were Nora."

"Then if she escaped, she'd either think she was Nora, or sound so crazy no one would believe her," Miles finished.

Caitlin went white. "And they didn't."

He nodded. "Meanwhile, Nora set the wheels in motion. She'd already stolen your parents' trust fund. She wanted to take over your life, Caitlin, your identity. Then her baby would have a father. So she replaced you in your marriage."

A strangled sound erupted from Caitlin. Miles saw the confusion on her face. The horror. The pain.

Her sister had betrayed her. Had tried to assume her life, her marriage. Had tried to destroy Caitlin.

Miles mentally recounted details of the past few weeks as the extent of Nora's duplicity hit him. He and Caitlin had met, fallen in love, married. All of it had been true. Then she had met her sister one night, three days after their wedding, and she'd been drugged and imprisoned in the hospital, just as she'd claimed when she'd escaped and come to him seeking help. She had been a victim.

Three days after their wedding—that night he'd sensed Caitlin had changed. She wasn't the same woman. She'd been cold, unemotional, hadn't made love to him with the same tenderness.

Not the way she had the night before. Not the way she had when they'd married.

Caitlin had sipped wine occasionally. Nora had been the scotch drinker....

God. He stood, shock rocking through him. He had slept with Nora, he had betrayed his vows without even knowing it. Tension knotted his shoulders. But he *had* known. He'd known she was different. It just had never occurred to him that she wasn't his wife because he didn't know of Nora's existence.

His gaze met hers. This woman was his missing wife. She had been hurt so much, was an innocent in all this. She hadn't left him, hadn't cheated on him.

So ultimately Hollinsby's experiment had failed.

Because she had returned to him. They'd connected immediately, had fallen in love all over again. When they'd made love the night before, he'd sensed that he loved her, that she'd felt right in his arms, the way she had in the beginning.

SHOCK IMMOBILIZED Caitlin as memories filtered through her despair. She'd phoned Nora and begged her to attend the wedding, but her sister had been jealous. Hadn't had time. Caitlin had been so hurt she hadn't told Miles about her sister. She'd attempted one too many times to reconcile with Nora, but Nora kept pushing her away. Then three days after she and Miles had married, Nora had phoned. Out of the blue, she'd asked Caitlin to meet her in town at the Steel Toe. They had ordered drinks, and she'd told Nora about Miles. She'd hoped Nora would be happy for her. But Nora had been angry, had confessed that she was pregnant, and they'd argued.

Nora wanted to have an abortion, but Caitlin had begged her not to. She'd even offered to take the baby and raise it. After that, the world had gone black because her sister had drugged her.

Pain splintered through her at the extent of her sister's duplicity. Nora had hated her.

Nora had signed her into that psych ward to be treated like a lab animal. And while Caitlin was fighting for her sanity and her life, Nora had pretended to be Miles's wife.

Her gaze latched on to his. She saw the same recognition, the horror in his eyes, as the truth dawned between them. Her sister had been diabolical, had slept with Miles, had betrayed him, then screamed that she wanted out of the marriage. She'd gone to the Steel Toe and met up with strange men at the same time she pretended to be married.

Her head hurt, her chest ached from the pressure, and nausea suddenly rose in her throat. Tears blurred her vision, choking her.

"I'm sorry, Caitlin," Hollinsby said in a muffled voice. "But I had to save my reputation. And I…loved your sister."

A sob caught in Caitlin's throat. Miles reached for her, but her head swam with emotions. She couldn't breathe, much less speak, couldn't process the fact that Nora had hated her so much, that she'd stolen her husband from her.

That Nora had locked her away, then slept with Miles while she was fighting off drugs and nightmarish treatments on that island. That if Miles had caught on sooner, he might have realized she was missing.

Miles cleared his throat, reached for her, his face a blur of turbulent emotions. She wanted to hold him, to whisper that she still loved him, but bile climbed into her throat cutting off her words. While she'd been struggling in that hospital, praying someone would find her, he had slept with her sister.

She jumped up and ran from the room, her heart breaking.

MILES DARTED THROUGH the door to chase Caitlin, but Brown stopped him in the hallway. "Give her a minute," Brown said. "She's had quite a shock, it'll take time for her to absorb what her sister and this maniac did to her."

And that he'd slept with Nora. Even though he hadn't known it, now she had that image emblazoned in her memory, would she ever be able to erase it? Had her twin really driven them apart with her diabolical plan? No…he couldn't allow her to destroy the best thing that had ever happened to him.

"Hollinsby mentioned that swingers Web site," Brown said. "That has to be the link. Let me call my guys and see if they've uncovered anything."

Brown punched in a number and explained their findings to Agent Adams. When he hung up, he turned to Miles. "She was at the diner, just finished questioning Reverend Perry. She should be here in a minute."

"I can't believe this is happening," Miles said.

"Listen, Monahue, I know you're upset, but you have to focus. We must stop The Carver."

Miles glanced down the hall toward the ladies' room, his pulse pounding. Brown was right. Caitlin needed time. And they needed to find this killer.

But he couldn't stand not to be with her. He had to explain, convince her that he wanted her, that he had never stopped loving her. That sleeping with Nora had meant nothing to him. That the night before, he'd thought it was her, that she'd found her way back to him.

Agent Adams burst into the front office. "I have a printout of all the members of that Web site," she said as she dumped papers onto Miles's desk. "I also cross-referenced contacts the seven victims made online and have copies of their e-mail correspondence so we can search for a connection."

"We need a name," Brown said. "It's got to be here."

"What about that new preacher, Reverend Perry?" Miles asked.

Agent Adams shook her head. "He was delivering sermons the night of each of the murders."

Anxiety pulled at Miles's shoulders. "Let me check on Caitlin. She's in the ladies' room."

"Caitlin?" Agent Adams asked. "I just saw her outside talking with the medical examiner."

"That's odd," Brown said. "He didn't come inside."

Miles ran to the door and searched the parking lot, but Mullins's dark sedan was nowhere to be seen. Christ, what was happening?

Something nagged at the back of his mind, and panic streaked through him. He rushed to check the restroom, but it was empty. Where in the hell was Caitlin? Had she left with Mullins? But why—

His cell phone trilled and he connected it, praying it was Caitlin.

"Monahue?"

"Sheriff, this is Father Flemming."

"Father, I'm busy right now, unless this—"

"It's urgent. I called to warn you." Father Flemming rasped. "He was just here. He…said he's going after another woman. He believes he's driven by the spirit."

"Who the hell is he?" Miles barked. "Is it Reverend Perry?"

"I can't say—"

Details slammed into Miles's consciousness. The handwriting. The way the killer had written the letter *A*.

Arthur Mullins—he'd seen the medical examiner's signature on his reports. He slanted his *A*'s just like the killer.

He gripped the phone so hard his fingers went numb. "It's Dr. Mullins, isn't it?"

Father Flemming hesitated.

"For God's sake, tell me!"

"Yes. He came to confession after he killed the Collier twin and Tina Hollinsby. I tried to persuade him to turn himself in, but he's convinced he's ridding the world of sinners."

His breath caught in his chest as he spun toward the two agents. "Mullins is The Carver. And he has Caitlin!"

Miles thanked the priest, then disconnected the call. "Good God, where would he take her?"

"You're right," Agent Adams said as she skimmed the handout and evidence file. "Mullins's handwriting matches, and there's a notation for an A. Carver who logged on to the Web site."

"You two check the morgue," Miles said. "I'll check Mullins's house." He punched in the local judge's number to request a search warrant as he sprinted toward his car. The judge agreed, and he hung up and phoned his deputy. His tires squealed as he roared from the parking lot.

"Start combing the town and foothills of the mountains," Miles told his deputy. "Look for any deserted cabins where Mullins might have taken Caitlin."

His deputy agreed, and Miles accelerated, sweat trickling down his neck as he raced toward Mullins's house.

He hadn't just found Caitlin to lose her to this twisted killer.

THE DARKNESS SWALLOWED HER. Caitlin tried to open her eyes, but the throbbing in her temple sent pain splintering through her, and made her dizzy. Where was she? What had happened?

The last hour rolled back in muted pieces. She'd run to the ladies' room, an emotional mess, then the medical examiner had stuck a gun against her back and forced her out the back door to his car. He must have whacked her on the back of the head, too, because she'd lost consciousness.

Pinpoints of white light stabbed her eyes as she searched the darkness. A sharp stone jabbed her side, and the ground below her was cold and hard. The faint *drip, drip* of water trickling shattered the silence. Cold seeped through her.

She must be in a cave of some sort.

Her breath lodged in her throat, and she tried to move, but her hands and feet were bound, and he'd stripped her naked.

Icy terror clutched her. Dr. Mullins had killed Nora— he was The Carver.

And now he was going to kill *her.*

A cry tore from her, but she tamped it down, forcing air through her mouth so she could think. Then the faint sound of his breathing reverberated through the air.

Choppy. Erratic. Another wave of horror swept through her.

Another noise sliced through the tension. The sound of a knife being sharpened against stone.

He had kept Nora for three weeks. How long had he kept the others?

How long would he keep her before he made her join her sister in the grave?

Chapter Eighteen

Miles stormed into Mullins's house, his nerves strung so tightly he thought his lungs would explode. Mullins, the damn medical examiner. A man who carved bodies up on a daily basis as his job.

They hadn't once thought to look at him as a suspect.

No wonder they hadn't found any evidence leading to the killer. Mullins had buried it. And he remembered now that Mullins had taken several trips this past year, supposedly to medical conventions. If he checked, he'd probably confirm that Mullins was in Savannah and Atlanta at the times of the other murders.

The man had been right in front of Miles the entire time, at every crime scene, at the conferences to discuss the crimes, at Nora's funeral.

Miles searched each of the four rooms of the small house, not surprised that the place was tidy and that it smelled of bleach. If Mullins had committed any of the crimes here, he'd cleaned up after himself, gotten rid of any evidence.

And he and Caitlin weren't here.

He rummaged through the desk drawer, looking for information on a second house or cabin he owned. Instead, he discovered a small wooden box carved with Mullins's initials on the top—inside he found seven wedding rings.

Miles's heart clenched as he recognized the simple gold band he'd given Caitlin.

Where the hell had the sicko taken his wife?

He punched Brown's number. "Monahue. He's not at the house."

"He's not at the morgue, either."

Terror clawed at Miles, launching him back weeks to the day Caitlin had first disappeared. But this time was worse—this time he knew she loved him, and that she hadn't run away. That a madman had her.

And if he didn't find her, she'd end up like her sister.

His phone beeped, indicating he had another call. "Let me get that, Brown. It's my deputy."

He clicked over. "Monahue."

"Sheriff, did you find them?"

"No. He's not at his cabin or the morgue."

"Listen, I pulled up some maps of the area. There's a series of caves near that creek where the other two victims were found. Right at the base of Devil's Ravine."

Miles had no idea if that was where the man had gone, but he had to look. "I'm on my way."

"I'll meet you there."

"No, keep searching around town for any empty cabins." He disconnected, and punched Brown's number again as he raced to his SUV. Brown agreed to meet him in the ravine.

Miles gunned the engine and sped around the mountain. His tires skidded on black ice as he rounded the curves, and he downshifted, gears grinding. Wind whistled through the branches of the shivering trees. Storm clouds darkened the sky and rumbled, threatening sleet. The ride barely took ten minutes, although it felt like hours. He parked as close to the ravine as he could, climbed out and ran down the embankment. Gravel and rocks pinged and rained downward, and twigs snapped beneath his weight. When he reached the bottom, he scanned the area, and spotted a rock indentation that resembled a cave. He checked for footprints, anything to indicate someone had recently been there, but didn't see anything suspicious. Still, he checked the cave, his weapon drawn as he forged into the darkness. Cold air assaulted him as he entered, and he paused, his senses alert, but he heard nothing. He shined his flashlight around the space though, searching.

Dammit. The cave was empty.

He rushed out, then scanned the brush and trees, searching for another cave nearby. Several broken tree limbs and branches had fallen into a pile, and he headed toward it. He slanted the flashlight toward the ground and found muddy footprints at the mouth of the cave. Another spot looked like blood.

His stomach convulsed. Caitlin couldn't be dead. God, no…

He approached cautiously, his gun drawn, his ears alert for sounds. A gust of wind rustled the trees, and a wild animal howled in the distance.

Seconds later, he slipped into the hollowed-out black opening. The ping of water dripping from the walls broke the silence, then the low cry of Caitlin's voice pleading for Mullins to release her echoed off the stone walls.

"DO NOT WORRY about your clothes, the field lilies do not worry about theirs…." Mullins looked up from the Bible he'd been reading, then brought the knife down and traced it over Caitlin's bare breasts, mimicking the letter *A* that he'd carved into his other victims' chests.

"Please," she whispered. "Let me go. You took my sister—"

"Your sister betrayed her vows, she slept with others. And you are sleeping with your sister's husband."

"No, I'm Caitlin, I married Miles. I never betrayed him."

A drop of blood surfaced, pooling on her pale skin, and her sob wrenched the air as he brought the knife upward, preparing to pierce her heart with it.

Suddenly a loud roar reverberated off the stone cold walls, and through the darkness, a shadow emerged, large and powerful.

Miles.

He jumped Mullins from behind, ripped the knife from his hand with a vicious growl, and threw him to the ground. Mullins bellowed, and Miles grunted, then pounded him with his fists. They rolled sideways, fighting and cursing.

Caitlin struggled with the bindings, but her arms were raw and bleeding, and she was tied down so tightly to the stones that she couldn't move. The faint light from the outside disappeared, and despair filled her as the black emptiness swallowed her again.

Fighting sounds cut into the night. Grunts and groans. Bones breaking. A gunshot pinged off a rock, then another, and her heart slammed against her ribs.

"Miles!"

Dear God, please. Mullins couldn't have killed him.

A low moan followed, then silence. A deafening silence. Her life flashed in front of her. Sketchy memories.

Her and Nora as kids when Nora still loved her. The day she'd married Miles. The kiss that followed.

A sob of terror and grief mounted inside her and overflowed. "Please, Miles, don't leave me," she whispered.

A hulking shadow loomed toward her. Mullins. She screamed and kicked, but the ropes tore at her skin. He had a knife. The silhouette of it radiated off the stone wall, then he brought it downward and lunged toward her.

She screamed, and another shot rang through the air. Mullins grunted, his eyes going wide with pain and shock. Then his body convulsed, and he collapsed onto the dirt. Blood spurted from his mouth and nose as he gagged and clawed at the ground. A strangled sound was ripped from him, and he wheezed a shaky breath, then his body went rigid.

She tore her eyes away from him and searched the blinding darkness for Miles. He had to survive. They had gone through too much not to be together.

Then she saw his shadow. Heard his breathing. He staggered toward her, grabbed the knife from the dirt and ripped away her bindings. She was shaking all over, crying and choking out his name as he dragged her into his arms, crushed her to his chest, and held her.

Chapter Nineteen

Miles shook with emotions as he cradled Caitlin in his arms. God, he'd almost lost her. She sobbed against him, and he ripped off his coat, wrapped it around her, then crooned soothing, nonsensical words to her as he rocked her back and forth. "Shh, it's over now, Caitlin, I've got you, honey."

Distraught, he finally pulled away slightly, enough to check her for injuries. The sight of her naked body fired his rage. And blood dotted her breasts… He growled and a tremor tore through him.

"Let me call an ambulance."

"No, I'm okay," she whispered.

The hell she was.

Shouting erupted outside. Agent Brown and Agent Adams.

"In here!" he yelled.

They rushed in and surrounded Mullins.

"I need to get her to the hospital," Miles said.

Brown gave him a clipped nod. "Go ahead and take her. We'll stay here and tie things up."

Miles muttered thanks, then swept Caitlin into his arms and strode up the ravine to his car. He grabbed the blanket he kept in the back and wrapped it around her, flipped on his siren, then sped toward the hospital. Caitlin curled into the blanket and leaned against him, her body trembling as she clung to him.

The next hour was chaotic as he rushed her into the E.R. He didn't want to leave her, but she assured him she'd be okay while the doctors and nurses examined her. He phoned his deputy and filled him in, then checked in with Brown. A CSI unit and the coroner from Black Mountain were at the crime scene already.

Tomorrow the story would be all over the papers. The headlines would rock the community.

Secret Society of Swingers found in the sleepy little mountain town of Raven's Peak. Medical examiner turns out to be The Carver.

Sheriff's wife alive—but suffers from an identity crisis caused by a mad scientist.

HE PACED THE WAITING ROOM, anxious to see Caitlin. Even though the killer was caught, Hollinsby was in jail and she was safe, he couldn't stand for her to be away from him. Every second that ticked by, he feared he would lose her again.

That when she recovered from the shock of the ordeal of her attack, and her hurt over her sister's betrayal, she would feel as if he'd betrayed her, too.

Could she ever forget the fact that he had actually slept with her sister? And could she forgive him for not figuring out the truth sooner?

AN HOUR LATER, the doctors confirmed that Caitlin was fine. Hollinsby was in jail. Mullins was dead. She was safe now.

She could go home if she wanted.

But where was home?

Miles stood in the corner of the room by the window, his back to her, his shoulders squared, his Ray-Bans in place, his expression guarded. He must hate her for what she and her sister had put him through.

She still couldn't believe all that had happened.

Agent Brown confirmed that they had irrefutable evidence proving that Mullins had killed all seven victims. Hollinsby had admitted that his coworker, Dr. Omar White, from the research center in Black Mountain, had panicked when Caitlin had escaped and had hired someone to try to kill her. The sniper had shot at them in Savannah when they'd left Nighthawk Island. Brown had agents searching for White and the sniper now.

They'd also discovered a journal that detailed Mullins's thoughts, and proved he was psychotic. He had suffered terrible abuse as a child. His father had been a mortician and a religious fanatic, and had locked him in a coffin as punishment for misbehavior.

Mullins had also killed his mother because she had been a whore. As an adult, he studied religion, but his wife cheated on him and he snapped. After that, it became his mission to rid the world of adulterers.

He'd come after Caitlin thinking she had seduced her sister's husband.

At last, everyone filed out, leaving her alone with her husband. She had no idea what to say. What to do. Her memories slowly crept back, but she realized she might need therapy to help her sort through the tangled web that Dr. Hollinsby had created.

Miles walked over to her and brushed a thumb along her hand, tentative. Tender.

"I'll take you home now…or wherever you want to go, Caitlin." His voice sounded gruff.

She twisted the sheet between her fingers. "I don't know where home is anymore."

He squeezed her hand, turbulent emotions filling his eyes. "It's where your heart is. Listen to it, and it'll lead you in the right direction."

She had to swallow back a sob. "My heart is with you, Miles, but—"

His breath rushed out, and he tensed, waiting. Praying. Hoping. "But what?"

"But how could you ever forgive me? Forgive Nora? Forget what's happened?"

He scrubbed a hand over the back of his neck, his jaw tight. "You did nothing wrong, Caitlin. You didn't betray me, *you* were a victim."

"And so were you." Her voice broke. "I should have told you about Nora, b-but I was so hurt when she refused to attend our wedding, that I couldn't bear to talk about her. I had no idea she hated me so much, no idea she'd try to steal my life, or you…"

"She was disturbed, Caitlin. I know that hurts, but it wasn't your fault." He sat down beside her on the hospital bed, and gently brushed her hair from her cheek.

"But if I'd understood how she felt, maybe I could have helped her. We were so close once."

"Shh. Don't blame yourself. Nora died because she became involved with that swingers group, because she deceived you."

Caitlin glanced down at his fingers, to the wedding

ring he still wore. He hadn't removed it even when he thought she'd betrayed him.

Then to her ringless finger. "Nora will always be there between us."

"Because you can't forget that I slept with her?" he asked in a low voice.

Hearing him say the words aloud only drove the knife of pain deeper into her heart. "You didn't know, Miles, I can't blame you—"

"But I did know."

She jerked her gaze up, stunned, her heart thrashing in her chest. What was he talking about?

"That night when you went missing," he said, his voice thick with emotions, "when Nora came home in your place and I touched her, when we made love—"

"Please, stop, Miles…." She covered her ears, unable to hear the details, hating the image of the two of them together.

He gently eased her hands away, then removed his Ray-Bans. "I know this is difficult for you to hear, and dammit, it's hard for me to say, but we have to talk about it. You have to listen, then we can put it behind us."

Tears threatened, but she blinked them away. Could they?

He forced her to look at him. "I knew something was different that night. Wrong." Regret softened his tone to a husky whisper. "I just didn't understand what it was, but the love, the connection, it wasn't there, Caitlin. Not the way it had been when *we* made love."

Her chin quivered as she struggled to believe him.

"Don't you understand?" His voice rose in conviction. "I felt that same intense draw again when you returned, and so did you. I tried to fight it because I was hurt, and then because I thought you were Nora, but we were drawn together again because we were meant to be together." He hesitated, reached for her hands, pulled them into his. "That's why we made love again, not because I fell for your sister. Because deep down on some subconscious level, I knew it was you." He tipped her chin up with his thumb, made her look into his eyes again, then kissed her fingers. "Even Hollinsby and his crazy research experiment, and Nora and her deceit couldn't destroy what we have together."

She saw the truth then. He'd shed his glasses, his defenses, had put not only his life, but his heart and soul on the line. His feelings were so stark, raw, his eyes filled with love and fear, that he didn't try to hide.

His wedding ring glinted beneath the light, and her heart squeezed again. He hadn't removed it, because he'd never given up on them. He'd taken care of her fish while she was gone. And he'd helped her, even when she was so confused and lost she didn't know her own name. He was a strong, tough man, the one she wanted by her side.

She couldn't give up, either.

He brushed a kiss across her mouth, then reached inside his pocket and opened his palm. A charm bracelet lay in the center. It was silver, a simple pattern with two tiny hearts melded together.

Déjà vu struck her as she picked it up and fingered the hearts. Then her gaze met his.

"You kept it?"

He smiled, hope lighting his eyes. "You remember?"

She nodded and wiped at her tears. "We were walking together, hand in hand, window-shopping in town," she whispered. "Then we spotted this bracelet in that little mom-and-pop jewelry store. You said it reminded you of kids carving hearts into trees with their initials inside." She glanced up at him, studied his face, willed the rest of the memory to surface. Her heart overflowed with love for him when it did. "You dragged me inside and insisted I try it on. Then you bought it for me and fastened it around my wrist."

"And you had tears in your eyes."

"Because you told me you loved me." She squeezed his hand. "And I promised to wear it forever."

"I do love you, Caitlin." He leaned forward, so close his breath brushed her cheek. So close her belly twisted with desire. "It's always been you." He kissed her on the lips. "Only you."

She slipped her arms around his neck, angled her head and closed her eyes as he claimed her mouth again. "I love you, too, Miles."

The kiss was sweet, tender, erotic, full of promises, deepening as she opened to him. She no longer had the wedding ring he had given her. And now that Nora had worn it, and the killer had tainted it, she didn't want it back. Besides, she didn't need a ring to tell her that she belonged to Miles, that she was his wife.

The charm bracelet with the melded hearts said it all— their hearts were one, beating together, as they would forever.

* * * * *

Don't miss Rita Herron's next Harlequin Intrigue
FORCE OF THE FALCON,
coming in December, 2006.
And in February 2007, be sure to pick up
her latest novel from HQN Books,
SAY YOU LOVE ME.

Set in darkness beyond the ordinary world.
Passionate tales of life and death.
With characters' lives ruled by laws the everyday world
can't begin to imagine.

Introducing NOCTURNE, *a spine-tingling*
new line from Silhouette Books.

The thrills and chills begin with
UNFORGIVEN by Lindsay McKenna

Plucked from the depths of hell, former military sharp-shooter Reno Manchahi was hired by the government to kill a thief, but he had a mission of his own. Descended from a family of shape-shifters, Reno vowed to get the revenge he'd thirsted for all these years. But his mission went awry when his target turned out to be a powerful seductresss, Magdalena Calen Hernandez, who risked everything to battle a potent evil. Suddenly, Reno had to transform himself into a true hero and fight the enemy that threatened them all. He had to become a Warrior for the Light....

Turn the page for a sneak preview of
UNFORGIVEN by Lindsay McKenna.
On sale September 26, wherever books are sold.

Chapter 1

One shot...one kill.

The sixteen-pound sledgehammer came down with such fierce power that the granite boulder shattered instantly. A spray of glittering mica exploded into the air and sparkled momentarily around the man who wielded the tool as if it were a weapon. Sweat ran in rivulets down Reno Manchahi's drawn, intense face. Naked from the waist up, the hot July sun beating down on his back, he hefted the sledgehammer skyward once more. Muscles in his thick forearms leaped and biceps bulged. Even his breath was focused on the boulder. In his mind's eye, he pictured Army General Robert Hampton's fleshy, arrogant fifty-year-old features on the rock's surface. Air exploded from between his lips as he brought the avenging hammer down. The boulder pulverized beneath his funneled hatred.

One shot...one kill...

Nostrils flaring, he inhaled the dank, humid heat and drew it deep into his massive lungs. Revenge allowed Reno to endure his imprisonment at a U.S. Navy brig near San Diego, California. Drops of sweat were flung in all directions as the crack of his sledgehammer claimed a third stone victim. Mouth taut, Reno moved to the next boulder.

The other prisoners in the stone yard gave him a wide berth. They always did. They instinctively felt his simmering hatred, the palpable revenge in his cinnamon-colored eyes, was more than skin-deep.

And they whispered he was different.

Reno enjoyed being a loner for good reason. He came from a medicine family of shape-shifters. But even this secret power had not protected him—or his family. His wife, Ilona, and his three-year-old daughter, Sarah, were dead. Murdered by Army General Hampton in their former home on USMC base in Camp Pendleton, California. Bitterness thrummed through Reno as he savagely pushed the toe of his scarred leather boot against several smaller pieces of gray granite that were in his way.

The sun beat down upon Manchahi's naked shoulders, grown dark red over time, shouting his half-Apache heritage. With his straight black hair grazing his thick shoulders, copper skin and broad face with high cheekbones, everyone knew he was Indian. When he'd first arrived at the brig, some of the prisoners taunted him and called him Geronimo. Something strange happened to Reno during his fight with the name-calling prisoners. Leaning down after he'd won the scuffle, he'd snarled into each of their bloodied faces that if they were going to call him anything, they would call him *gan,* which was the Apache word for *devil.*

His attackers had been shocked by the wounds on their faces, the deep claw marks. Reno recalled doubling his fist as they'd attacked him en masse. In that split second, he'd gone into an altered state of consciousness. In times of danger, he transformed into a jaguar. A deep, growling sound had emitted from his throat as he defended himself in the three-against-one fracas. It all happened so fast that he thought he had imagined it. He'd seen his hands morph into a forearm and paw, claws extended. The slashes left on the three men's faces after the fight told him he'd begun to shape-shift. A fist made bruises and swelling; not four perfect, deep claw marks. Stunned and anxious, he hid the knowledge of what else he was from these prisoners. Reno's only defense was to make all the prisoners so damned scared of him and remain a loner.

Alone. Yeah, he was alone, all right. The steel hammer swept downward with hellish ferocity. As the granite groaned in protest, Reno shut his eyes for just a moment. Sweat dripped off his nose and square chin.

Straightening, he wiped his furrowed, wet brow and looked into the pale blue sky. What got his attention was the startling cry of a red-tailed hawk as it flew over the brig yard. Squinting, he watched the bird. Reno could make out the rust-colored tail on the hawk. As a kid growing up on the Apache reservation in Arizona, Reno knew that all animals that appeared before him were messengers.

Brother, what message do you bring me? Reno knew one had to ask in order to receive. Allowing the sledge-hammer to drop to his side, he concentrated on the hawk who wheeled in tightening circles above him.

Freedom! the hawk cried in return.

Reno shook his head, his black hair moving against his broad, thickset shoulders. *Freedom? No way, Brother. No way.* Figuring that he was making up the hawk's shrill message, Reno turned away. Back to his rocks. Back to picturing Hampton's smug face.

Freedom!

* * * * *

*Look for UNFORGIVEN by Lindsay McKenna,
the spine-tingling launch title from
Silhouette Nocturne ™.
Available September 26, wherever books are sold.*

nocturne™

Save $1.⁰⁰ off

your purchase of any Silhouette® Nocturne™ novel.

Receive $1.00 off

any Silhouette® Nocturne™ novel.

Available wherever books are sold, including most bookstores, supermarkets, drugstores and discount stores.

Coupon expires December 1, 2006. Redeemable at participating retail outlets in the U.S. only. Limit one coupon per customer.

5 65373 00076 2   (8100) 0 11265

SNCOUPUS

nocturne™

Save $1.00 off

your purchase of any Silhouette® Nocturne™ novel.

Receive $1.00 off

any Silhouette® Nocturne™ novel.

Available wherever books are sold, including most bookstores, supermarkets, drugstores and discount stores.

Coupon expires December 1, 2006. Redeemable at participating retail outlets in Canada only. Limit one coupon per customer.

52607136

SNCOUPCDN

SAVE UP TO $30! SIGN UP TODAY!

INSIDE *Romance*

The complete guide to your favorite
Harlequin®, Silhouette® and Love Inspired® books.

✓ Newsletter ABSOLUTELY FREE! No purchase necessary.

✓ Valuable coupons for future purchases of Harlequin,
  Silhouette and Love Inspired books in every issue!

✓ Special excerpts & previews in each issue. Learn about all
  the hottest titles before they arrive in stores.

✓ No hassle—mailed directly to your door!

✓ Comes complete with a handy shopping checklist
  so you won't miss out on any titles.

- -

SIGN ME UP TO RECEIVE INSIDE ROMANCE ABSOLUTELY FREE
(Please print clearly)

Name

Address

City/Town   State/Province   Zip/Postal Code

(098 KKM EJL9)

**Introducing an exciting appearance
by legendary
New York Times bestselling author**

DIANA PALMER

HEARTBREAKER

He's the ultimate bachelor…
but he may have just met
the one woman to change his ways!

Join the drama in the story of a confirmed
bachelor, an amnesiac beauty and their
unexpected passionate romance.

"Diana Palmer is a mesmerizing storyteller
who captures the essence of what
a romance should be."—*Affaire de Coeur*

Heartbreaker *is available from Silhouette Desire
in September 2006.*

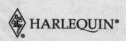

INTRIGUE

COMING NEXT MONTH

#945 RED ALERT by Jessica Andersen
Corporate mogul Erik Falco is drawn to acquiring a new medical breakthrough from Boston General Hospital before his competitors. But could Dr. Megan Corning also be part of the deal?

#946 CHAIN REACTION by Rebecca York
Security Breach
When an explosion exposes Gage Darnell to a dangerous chemical, he discovers he's acquired the ability to manipulate matter with his mind. But on the run and looking to reconnect with his estranged wife, Lily, will he be powerless to change hers?

#947 BABY JANE DOE by Julie Miller
The Precinct
An unsolvable case. An I.A. investigator with a keen mind to keep their public love private. And a vicious stalker with all the answers. All in a day's work for KCPD commissioner Shauna Cartwright.

#948 FOOTPRINTS IN THE SNOW by Cassie Miles
He's a Mystery
When a freak blizzard delivers Shana Parisi into the arms of sergeant Luke Rawlins, she's swept into a secret mission of the utmost importance and a love that transcends time.

#949 ISLAND IN THE FOG by Leona Karr
Eclipse
Searching for her missing sister on Greystone Island, Ashley Davis finds herself side by side with police officer Brad Taylor, who's investigating multiple deaths in the wealthy Langdon family. The family her sister worked for.

#950 COVERT CONCEPTION by Delores Fossen
Neither Rick Gravari nor Natalie Sinclair knew they were part of an experiment to produce genetically improved babies until Natalie unexpectedly becomes pregnant. But even if these rivals unveil this vast conspiracy, can they become the perfect parents?

www.eHarlequin.com

HICNM0906